ANGELINA
SHOWDOWN

Other books by Kent Conwell:

Death in the Distillery
Gunfight at Frio Canyon
The Riddle of Mystery Inn
An Eye for an Eye
Skeletons of the Atchafalaya
A Hanging in Hidetown
Galveston
The Gambling Man
Red River Crossing
A Wagon Train for Brides
Friday's Station
Sidetrip to Sand Springs
The Alamo Trail
Blood Brothers
The Gold of Black Mountain
Glitter of Gold
The Ghost of Blue Bone Mesa
Texas Orphan Train
Painted Comanche Tree
Valley of Gold
Bumpo, Bill, and the Girls
Wild Rose Pass
Cattle Drive to Dodge

ANGELINA SHOWDOWN

AVALON BOOKS
NEW YORK

© Copyright 2004 by Kent Conwell
Library of Congress Catalog Card Number: 2004091859
ISBN 0-8034-9680-X
Published by Thomas Bouregy & Co., Inc.
160 Madison Avenue, New York, NY 10016

PRINTED IN THE UNITED STATES OF AMERICA
ON ACID-FREE PAPER
BY HADDON CRAFTSMEN, BLOOMSBURG, PENNSYLVANIA

To my daughter, Susan. I'm proud of you.
When life really gets tough, you hang in there.
And to my wife, Gayle, who always manages to keep
me on the straight and narrow, I love you.

Chapter One

Maybe I should have listened to my crusty old partner when he warned me that nothing was as simple as it looked. Truth is, I didn't figure it would take a genius to pick up two youngsters at the Union Pacific railway terminal in Kansas City, load us all on a stage, and sit back for the seven hundred miles of jostling and bouncing to the Box D ranch on the Angelina River in East Texas.

But, I didn't listen.

My troubles began when my partner, Twitch, and I couldn't find the children at the train station in Kansas City. If I'd had any sense, I would have realized that that was just the beginning of our problems. But I didn't have any more sense than a loaf of sourdough bread, and I barged headlong into enough trouble to last me a lifetime.

My partner, Twitch Mabry, who could have passed

for a dried-up mesquite fence post outfitted in buck-skins, added new definition to the word, pessimistic. On the other hand, I would have to later agree that he just about summed up the year 1871 when he loosed an arc of tobacco juice and drawled, "Listen to me, Clay Morgan. You best figure that whatever can go wrong on this trip will." He shook his head, the edges of his thin lips pulled down in disgust. "I don't know why the old man don't go ahead and put them young-sters on the stage from Kansas City instead of having you and me pick them up."

We were the only two in the bunkhouse. The other wranglers were out tending the stock. Cookie was next door in the chuck house whipping up steak and gravy for supper.

I inhaled the pungent smell of coal oil and wood smoke that permeated the bunkhouse. Over the years, the odor had soaked into the log walls and into the clay chinking and daubing that sealed the spaces between the logs. I looked up from cleaning my six-gun, squinted through the cigarette smoke and gave Twitch a crooked grin. "Those youngsters are J.R.'s grandkids. He don't want them on the stagecoach by themselves, and if that's what he wants, that's what he'll get."

Twitch tore off another chunk of tobacco from the twist. "Yeah, but we just got back from Colorado two weeks ago. I still ain't recup—recov—ain't got over that cattle drive. How long was we gone . . . four months?"

Spinning the cylinder of my Colt, I chuckled. "Just

about." I eyed the golden double eagles inset in the handle grips, then seated the slick Navy Colt in my worn holster and rose to my feet. A fleeting grin ticked up the edges of my lips when I remembered Joe Sterling. Likely, I wouldn't see him for another few years.

I flicked the cigarette butt out the door onto the hardpan. "So, I reckon it's time to stop fussing and pack your warbags. J.R. says we need to ride out tomorrow. We got to meet the train from Philadelphia on August 15."

Twitch unfolded his lanky frame from his bunk with a healthy dose of cursing. "Right smack dab in the middle of the hottest time of the year, too."

Twitch was right about that. The next two weeks were so hot it took us a couple hours to cool our coffee in the mornings. Despite the scorching heat, we reached Kansas City on the fourteenth. We found a livery and made a deal to sell the animals along with the rigs. We planned to take the stagecoach back to the small village of Marion on the Angelina River in East Texas. From Marion, it was a short buggy ride down to Beaver Tail Valley and the Box D.

That night after a hot bath, a shave, and plenty of toilet water, we donned fresh duds and adjourned to the Red Dog Saloon.

I had only taken a sip from my glass when a hand clamped down on my shoulder. "Clay Morgan! You son-of-a-gun!"

I glanced in the mirror behind the bar and spotted

the grinning face of Joe Sterling behind me. I spun and gripped his hand. "Joe! What the Sam Hill you doing here? I figured you was headed back to Arizona Territory after we finished the cattle drive over to Denver."

Dressed in black with silver conchos on his black leather vest and a silver hatband on his black hat, he laughed and glanced down at the Navy Colt on my hip. "See you're still carrying the Colt."

I laid my hand on the butt and grinned. The Colt was a gift from Joe ten years earlier. I had pulled him out of the way of a stampede of Mexican steers that would have stomped him into a mudhole. He never would tell me what he paid for it, but he had a gold double eagle inset in each side of the grip. "Haven't been able to give it away. Tried, but no takers."

"Yeah. You bet." He laughed again and clapped Twitch on the shoulder. "How you doing, Twitch?"

Twitch just grunted and moved aside as Joe bellied up to the bar between Twitch and me. "Had to give up Arizona for the time being. Ran out of greenbacks. My full house wasn't strong enough for four ladies." He slapped a double eagle on the bar and ordered drinks. "I might ask you the same thing."

I explained our mission.

He whistled. "Sure am glad it ain't me that's got to ride back to Texas with two young'uns."

"Well, we aren't exactly looking forward to it," I admitted.

Joe laughed again and downed his drink in one

gulp. "Another one, barkeep," he shouted. "By the way, I saw Sunny yesterday."

"Sunny? What's he doing here?"

"Got a job driving a freight wagon. We didn't have time to talk much."

Joe Sterling was an amiable scoundrel who had always, at least in the ten or twelve years I had known him, tiptoed along the fine line between the law and outlaws. I couldn't help liking him although I disapproved of some of the shady deals in which he involved himself. He was always a conniver. Still, he'd never played me wrong.

But tonight, there was something different about Joe. I couldn't put my finger on it. There was a veneer of hardness beneath the affable demeanor. I glanced at Twitch, wondering if he had noticed anything different about Joe.

"Too bad you old boys got plans, Clay. I might have a sweet deal lined up over in Fort Leavenworth. Plenty of money to go around if it pays off."

Twitch and I looked at each other. I grinned crookedly. "Yep. Too bad, Joe. Maybe next time."

We grabbed a bottle and retired to a table in the rear of the saloon. Joe sat with his back to the wall, and I couldn't help noticing, his gun hand was never too far from his six-gun. His eyes swept the crowded room constantly.

For the next hour, we relived old times when we had both popped wild Mexican steers from the brush of South Texas before the war and drove them north to market. Then during the war we rode in Colonel

Thomas Waul's Texas Legion and ended up with
McClernand's Second Texas Lunette at the Railroad
Redoubt at the Battle of Vicksburg back in '63.

We were closer than most brothers for, more than
once we had been thrown out of some of the finest
saloons, stood off passels of Comanche, and dodged
thundering herds of stampeding cows. We lost count
the number of times we had saved each other's worthless skin.

Just before midnight, half-a-dozen rough-looking
owlhoots pushed through the batwing doors and
stomped up to the bar. They looked mean enough to
fight a rattlesnake and give him first bite. Joe stiffened,
then downed his drink and pushed back from the table.
"Well, Boys, it's been good rehashing old times. My
partners just came in. We got business to discuss." He
touched his fingers to the brim of his black hat, "Take
care."

We watched as he wove his way through the crowd
to the gang of toughs are the bar. Twitch muttered.
"Looks like rogue Injuns and flash floods might not
be the only danger we might run into going home."

I frowned at his cryptic remark.

He nodded to the jaspers at the bar. "Don't look
like he's learned to pick his friends any better since
we last saw him."

Frowning deeper, I rubbed my finger along the bone
behind my ear. "It sure don't."

Twitch sipped his drink. "I got me a bad feeling
that friend of yours is heading for big trouble."

I glanced at him. "Because of those jaspers?"

"Partly." He chewed on his bottom lip. "He just seemed different tonight. I don't know exactly what it was, but it wasn't the same as last time."

"You never liked Joe anyway."

Twitch pursed his lips. "Maybe not, but that ain't it."

For several moments, I studied Joe as the group of cowpokes huddled at the bar. Slender, dressed in black, he cut a figure to remember, but Twitch was right. Something was different about my old friend. He was skittish and antsy, like he was only one or two jumps ahead of the law.

During the night, heavy thunderstorms moved in, drenching the city and soaking the ground. We rose early and put ourselves around a breakfast of eggs, ham, steaming gravy, fresh baked biscuits, and hot coffee thicker than the old Missouri River just down the street.

Sitting by the rain-streaked window, we stared gloomily at the large puddles forming in the muddy street. Heads and tails drooping, forlorn-looking horses stood hipshot at the hitching rails.

"This ain't a fit day for nothing." Twitch drawled, sipping his coffee and taking a deep drag on his Bull Durham cigarette. A few burning strands of tobacco drifted down to the scarred tabletop.

I glanced at the Regulator clock sitting on a shelf behind the counter. "Almost seven," I said. "Another thirty minutes."

"If the blasted thing is on time."

An unbidden grin curled my lips.

"Now what?" Twitch frowned when I grinned, and when he did, the wrinkles on his face looked like a freshly plowed field.

Tilting my chair on its back legs, I chuckled. "In all our years together, Twitch, I've never heard you look on the good side of things even once. Now, just why in the Sam Hill is that? You got yourself any idea?"

His eyes narrowed, and he pursed his thin lips together while he studied me. With a sardonic drawl, he said, "Well, Boy, during our years together, as you said, I've seen you pull some mighty dumb stunts. I always managed to keep you from hurting yourself too bad. But I reckon I've sort of neglected your education, so maybe I ought to tell you the secret of life. I learned the hard way that if five things can go wrong, and you figure out a way to get around them, then a sixth will pop up before you can whistle 'Git Along Little Doggie.' " He tilted his chair back and gave me a smug grin.

I met his amused gaze. "You think that's the secret of life, huh?"

He rocked forward, the legs of his chair slapping the floor as he rose to his feet. He slipped into his slicker and buttoned it up tight. "Pardner, I know so. Now, let's stop our palavering and light a shuck on down to the train station."

The rain continued to fall, and the mud sucked at our boots as we sloshed across the street to the boardwalk fronting the clapboard buildings that lined the street. Early risers gathered in front of the few buildings with porches.

Huddling down in my slicker, I lowered my head into the pelting rain, the broad brim of my John B. Stetson deflecting the heavy drops.

We entered the station, dry as a tobacco can except from the knees down.

While I was shaking off the water like a Redtick Hound, Twitch grabbed my arm and nodded to the sign on the wall. He was excited. "Look at that, Clay. They got a train that runs south into Indian Territory."

I couldn't believe my eyes. Talk about luck. I smirked at Twitch. "What was that you said about everything going wrong?"

He just shrugged as I hurried up to the station agent. "Is that right?" I asked, pointing to the sign. "You have a train running down into Indian Territory?"

He nodded. "Yep."

"How far?"

"Right now, about a hundred miles."

Before I could say a word, he continued. "Except we lost a bridge two weeks back. Be another couple months before a train can get through, if then."

Behind me, Twitch snorted.

I looked around at him.

A crooked grin creased his angular face. "Well, Boy, what was that remark you just made about me?"

With a shrug, I replied. "All right. So you were right. If something can go wrong, it will." Shaking my head, I added, "Well, we're no worse off now than we were before. Soon as we pick up the youngsters, we'll head on down to the stage. One's pulling out at noon today."

We went out on the loading platform, which was covered, to await the train.

The good news was that despite the weather, the train was on time. The bad news was that we couldn't find the youngsters in the crowd of thirty or forty passengers who climbed down from the cars.

Twitch looked up and down the loading platform. "I sure didn't spot them kids, Clay."

With a sense of trepidation, I looked up through the windows into the passenger cars, expecting to see a couple young worried faces looking back. "Me neither. We had to miss them somewhere." I spotted the conductor making his way to the rear of one of the cars. "Stay here, and keep looking," I said, taking the stairs two at a time up into the car.

The conductor was coming out of the car as I reached the top of the steps. He pulled up. "Forget something?"

I shook my head. "Looking for two youngsters. Boy and girl. Twelve and nine. They came out from Philadelphia."

He held his hand just below shoulder high. "Blond-headed boy about this tall?"

"I've never seen them."

He nodded immediately. "Well, partner. They was two on the train, boy and girl. Names on the label pinned to them was Timothy William and Louisa Ann

Boykin. They was sure here, and am I glad this where they got off."

I was too relieved to inquire about his last remark. At least they were here somewhere. I glanced out the opposite window at the Missouri River rolling past. A cold chill shot up my spine. Could they have wandered out to the river?

"There they are now," the conductor exclaimed, pointing to a boy and girl standing in the middle of the platform looking in one direction down the plat-form. Behind them, Twitch was looking in the other.

I nearly broke my neck stumbling over my feet to get back to the platform.

I introduced Twitch and me.

They were both bright-eyed youngsters. Timothy about reached my shoulder, and Louisa was six or eight inches shorter. Clinging to her brother's arm, she avoided my eyes.

Timmy eyed me skeptically. "How do we know you are who you say?"

Well, that sort of backed me up a minute, but then I realized J.R. had given me the letter introducing us. "Can you read?"

He tilted his chin. With an arrogant curl on his lips, he replied, "Better than you probably."

Behind me, Twitch grunted.

That's when I remembered the conductor's remark about being glad the youngster had left the train. I held my temper and handed him the letter. He read it quickly, then handed it back to me. "My grandfather wrote that?"

"Yep." I folded the letter back into my pocket.

"Well, he doesn't spell very good."

My temper tugged at the reins, but I held it tight. Maybe the boy was just tired. I glanced at the girl. "What's your name, Missy?"

She buried her head in Timmy's arm. He replied for her. "Louisa. She doesn't talk much since father and mother died."

I glanced around at Twitch. He shrugged. "Well," I said. "Let's get your gear and head out for the stage."

"Wait." Timmy pointed down the platform to a man and woman. "That's Bill, the new schoolteacher in Beaver Tail Valley. We met on the train, and when I said where we were going, that's when we learned Bill is the new teacher. Maybe we'll go down there together."

I couldn't see what it would hurt. Chances were we'd all be on the stage together if Bill was going to Beaver Tail Valley. I glanced at the man and woman. She wore a gray cloak with a hood. He wore a tan suit with one of those black hats with a round top, a bowler, I think the fashion people called them. Funny, he didn't look much like a teacher.

In fact, he didn't look like he could last more than a couple weeks out here.

"Sure. Let's go down."

As we drew near, Timmy called out. "Hey, Bill."

Both the man and woman turned at the sound of his

voice. The man frowned, but the woman smiled warmly.

The young boy said, "Bill, I want you to meet Clay Morgan who my grandfather sent to pick us up."

I extended my hand toward the man in the bowler hat. To my surprise, the smiling woman stepped forward and took it. "I'm very pleased to meet you, Mr. Morgan."

All I could do was gape. I didn't even notice the jasper in the tan suit walking away as the rain turned into a fine mist.

Chapter Two

I had always had the knack to think on my feet. When a wild steer with a six-foot span of horns like needles jumped me in the South Texas brush, I knew instantly the right moves to make.

But now, I was floundering like the proverbial fish out of water. I was so flustered I forgot to shake her hand. I just held it. Finally, I found my voice. "But— But, I thought. . . ." My words trailed off, and I looked down helplessly at Timmy.

Bill laughed. "Everyone thinks the same thing." She shook my hand vigorously. "My real name's Wilhelmina Madison. My father always wanted a boy, so he shortened it to Bill. I've answered to it ever since."

After a few seconds, I managed to gather my wits. "Mighty pleased to know you, Ma'am."

With a petulant frown, she replied. "I prefer Bill, Mr. Morgan."

Behind me, Twitch grunted. "Well, I'll swear if that ain't something."

With a sheepish grin, I said, "If that's what you want. Bill it is. My name's Clay. This ugly galoot behind me is Twitch Mabry." For a moment, there was an awkward silence between us, but Timmy filled it up. "Is there someplace we can eat? I'm tired of the slop we had to eat on the train."

I looked at her. She shook her head. "I can't. I have to watch them unload my furniture for the train down to Denison, Texas."

"Denison?" Twitch and I exchanged looks. He cleared his throat. "Beg pardon, Ma'am, but there ain't no train to Denison. Tracks only go about halfway, and they're out for the next couple months according to the station attendant yonder."

Her slender face twisted in concern. She chewed on her bottom lip. "But, I can't leave the furniture behind. It's for my uncle's house and for the school."

My ears perked up. "Your uncle. You have an uncle in Beaver Tail Valley?"

"Yes, Hewitt Selby. You know him?"

Did I know him? "Yes, Ma'am. He owns The Running S, the ranch right next to the grandfather of these two youngsters—J.R. Drennan."

A comely smile erased the frown on her face. "Well, this is a small world. Who would have expected that I would run into my future next door neighbors in the middle of the country?"

Timmy interrupted with a whine, "I'm hungry."

Louisa just clung to his arm, her face buried in his sleeve.

"Hold your horses, Boy." I turned to Bill, feeling an obligation to help her since she was going to be a neighbor. "Why don't we have your furniture unloaded and arrange to haul it down to Beaver Tail Valley? You can take the stage with us, and let the furniture come behind."

Staring at the train, she shook her head. A strand of hair black as a raven's wing came out of the hood on her head. "No, thank you. I'll hire a wagon and man to take me and the furniture to Beaver Tail Valley."

That made no sense to me. We were only talking about furniture, not gold. "Ma'am . . . I mean, Bill, we can make it in half the time by stage. You've never ridden a wag—"

She smiled up at me. "Thank you for your concern, but I know what I have to do." Before I could even start into any further argument, she marched into the station, ordered her goods stacked on the platform, and inquired as to the nearest freight line.

In the meantime, Timmy kept complaining that he was hungry.

I turned to Twitch. "Take the youngsters over to the café and feed them something to keep him quiet. I'll try to talk sense to Bill."

My idea of talking sense and her idea of sense were at opposite ends of the world. Every objection I threw out, she countered. In a tone that left no uncertainty as to her intent, she said, "This furniture is too valuable to trust to someone I don't know." She paused, eyed me narrowly, than added in a resolute voice un-yielding to reason. "That's why I will ride along with the wagon all the way to Beaver Tail Valley."

I blew through my lips in frustration and rubbed my index finger along the bone behind my ear while I considered my next move. I couldn't let her stay here by herself. J.R. and Hewitt Selby had been neighbors for forty years. I couldn't leave Selby's niece up in Kansas all alone.

"All right . . . If that's what you want. I'm telling you, it's crazy, but if you're determined, I have a friend who drives for a local freight line. His name's Sunny. He's rode with me on a couple cattle drives up from Texas. I'd trust him with my life."

"What about my life?" She arched one eyebrow.

I couldn't tell if she was pulling my leg or not. I shrugged. "That, too."

"Good."

"You'll have to buy the wagon and horses and pay the driver down there and back unless Sunny wants to stay in Texas. I'll give him a job if he does."

"How much will all that cost me?"

I shrugged. "It's a seller's market up here. A six horse team and a light wagon ought to run about one-fifty to one seventy-five. Driver will cost about fifty a month." I hoped this might discourage her.

It didn't. "Sounds fair to me."

I paused, regretting what I was about to say, but knowing I had no choice. "If you're bound and deter-mined to go through with this fool trip, then I reckon

Twitch and me will ride along with you, that is, if you don't mind having a couple youngsters along."

She smiled up at me and pushed the hood off her head, revealing shiny black hair that hung to her shoulders. "I'd like the company. How long do you think the trip will take?"

"Hard to say. We were on the trail to Colorado with twenty-five hundred head of cows for about three months. I figure we can make better time than cows, so I'd guess a month or so with no problems."

The reaction I expected didn't come. Bill nodded slowly. "That isn't too bad. Might even be a pleasant trip."

Pleasant trip? No trip in the West was pleasant. I had more misgivings than a chicken has feathers about the trip we were to embark on with a tenderfoot like her, but they began to change when I saw her meet Sunny.

He was a broad-shouldered free black from Illinois. Instead of recoiling from him, she stepped forward and offered him her hand. And then as I watched her supervise the unloading and loading of her furniture, I realized she wasn't an Eastern-bred lady. Oh, she had the refinements, but the way she met problems head on was the way of the western woman.

Later, when we crossed the muddy street to the café, she didn't hesitate to lift her skirt above her ankles and pick her way through the mud.

Once in the café, Twitch's warning proved to be true once again. Louisa complained of stomach cramps. Bill knelt by her and gingerly touched her fingers to the girl's stomach. Louisa grimaced and doubled over.

Bill looked up at me. "We better take her to a doctor."

I nodded and glanced at Twitch, who said nothing. He just gave me a smug look that spoke volumes.

Fortunately, the girl's ailment was nothing more serious than a light case of food poisoning, picked up from food served aboard the train.

While the old doctor tended her, I peered through the window at the loaded wagon in the middle of the freight yard, the furniture covered with a white canvas tarp. Now I wasn't one of those connoisseurs of furniture, but for the life of me, I couldn't see why Bill was so set on those pieces. There was a round table with a middle pedestal about a foot thick, six chairs, a podium, a large mirror, a box of books, and naturally, her luggage.

Studying the items as they were loaded, I could see no reason for her to be so insistent on traveling with the furniture. No, sir. It didn't make sense, but then I was never too bright when it came to figuring out women.

So, I kept quiet about my concerns.

The doctor wanted to keep Louisa under observation overnight. "She can stay here," he announced, gesturing to the small room attached to the rear of his office.

Bill glanced at the wagon. "Isn't there someplace

we can put the wagon tonight so it will be safe? I'd hate to lose anything."

Twitch and I exchanged puzzled glances. "Safe? I reckon it'll be safe right there in the freight yard."

She shook her head adamantly. "Oh, no," she said sharply, too sharply. Quickly, she softened her voice. "I just mean, someplace indoors—a barn or something. Where I know it will be safe."

Now, I might not be too swift, but I'm not so dumb that I can't spot a goat in a flock of sheep. And right now, I had the sneaking feeling I was looking at a goat of some sort. I nodded. "Yes, Ma'am—I mean Bill. We can probably find a spot. Maybe the freight company has something."

The old doctor interrupted. "I've given the girl some *guaco* tea to help settle her stomach. That's about all we can do."

Bill frowned. "*Guaco* tea? What on earth is that?"

He grinned. "Stinkweed. It's right dandy for calming down the belly and intestines." He laid a hand on Louisa's cheek and looked around at Bill. "One of you can stay here with her tonight. Don't let her eat or drink nothing more than a few sips of tea. Otherwise," he added with a wry grin, "it'll come right back up. I'll stop by in the morning."

Bill nodded dutifully. "Yes, Doctor."

He nodded to the door. "I'll be in my office the rest of the day if you need me."

I spoke up. "How long do you reckon she'll be laid up, Doc?"

"Not long." He grunted. "Young'uns recuperate mighty fast. Give her a couple days."

Timmy shook his head. "Two days?" He glared at the doctor. "I'm not going to stay in this room for two days. It smells," he said with an arrogant curl to his lips.

"Timmy! Hush. Don't talk like that to the doctor," Bill exclaimed. "That isn't polite."

He glared at her, but remained silent, which was lucky for him. He didn't know it, but he had my dander up. I was ready to jam my hand down his throat and yank him inside out.

Twitch and I headed for the telegraph office where I sent word to J.R. Drennan about our change in plans. Instead of two weeks on the stage, the trip would take about a month. And, promising a letter with detailed explanations to follow, I reassured him the two youngsters were in good hands.

Bill remained in the back room of the doctor's office with Louisa and Timmy while Twitch and me went to see about finding someplace to park the wagon for the night. Fortunately, the rain had ceased.

"Sounds like a waste of time putting up that wagon at night. Ain't nothing going to happen where it is." Twitch complained.

I shrugged. "Maybe so, but if that's what it takes to make her feel better, that's what we'll do. Last thing I need is some woman complaining for seven hundred miles that I let some jasper run off with her furniture."

Twitch chuckled. "You tell her how dangerous it is on the trail?"

"She wouldn't listen."

"You should have made her listen. Everything from rogue Injuns to floods can pop up before you can blink an eye. You should have told her that."

I looked around at him. "You tell her. Maybe she'll listen to you."

Sunny Helms met us in the freight yard with a broad grin that revealed a set of white teeth contrasting sharply with his black skin. A free man, he hailed from Illinois, and the first thing I noticed about him when we met on the first trail drive was that he didn't talk like any of the black folks in our part of the country. He talked more like white folk. That was because he had come from up North, Twitch had explained. "Howdy, Clay. When do you reckon on moving out?"

I hooked my thumb over my shoulder. "Not for a couple days. The girl up and got herself sick. She's at the Doc's office. We're looking for a driver. You interested? I got a job for you on our ranch when we get there."

His grin grew wider. "Why not? I ain't cut out to load and unload freight all day. That's too much like work."

I laughed and nodded to the wagon. "The lady wants us to put her wagonload of furniture up for the night."

"Yep," drawled Twitch. "She's afraid somebody's going to run off with it."

"What about your freight barn?" I gestured to the large board and batten building at the back of the lot. "Can we push it in there for the night?"

Sunny shrugged his broad shoulders and shoved his battered slouch hat to the back of his head. "Don't see why not. We'll hitch up a team and back it in."

Sunny had a special kinship with animals, and I watched with appreciation as he hitched two grays to the wagon and promptly backed it in the barn.

That was when I heard the squeak in the back left wheel. "You hear that?" I looked up at Sunny on the seat of the wagon. "What?"

"Sounds like the back wheel needs greasing," Twitch offered.

Leaping lightly to the ground, Sunny said. "Then I reckon we best grease it. You old boys jack up the axle while I turn the animals back to the corral."

While I was jacking the axle with Twitch giving directions, Joe Sterling wandered in, a half-full bottle of old Orchard in his hand. "Saw you old boys come in here. Figured you might need something to warm your bellies." He took a slug and offered it to Twitch who promptly took his pull and passed it on to me. I took a slug and handed it back to Joe just as Sunny returned.

"I thought you was jacking up that wagon, Clay, not standing around drinking with this worthless cayuse here," Sunny said, grinning at Joe and taking the bottle from his hand.

"You know how it is, Sunny," Twitch said. "Clay

never could find decent folks to run with. That's why he's so no-account hisself."

We all laughed, and I went back to jacking up the axle. Sunny loosed the lock nut on the axle and wrestled the fifty-inch wheel off. Just as he gave a last tug, the jack slipped, and the wagon crashed to the ground. The axle snapped like a gunshot.

The furniture crashed to the bed of the wagon, and we heard the tinkle of broken glass.

Sunny rolled his eyes and cursed. I shook my head and reached for the bottle. "I can't believe it," I groaned. "I just can't believe all this." I could hear Bill now. We'd broken her precious mirror.

Twitch relieved me of the bottle, the contents of which were shrinking fast. "I always say, if something can go wrong, it will."

I glared at my old partner. "Blast it, Twitch. Do you always have to always keep reminding me of that?"

He wiped his thin lips with the back of his hand. "Nope." He paused, then added with a wicked gleam in his eyes. "But it do give me a right good deal of pleasure."

Sunny stepped forward. "Well, no sense in crying over what's done. Let's unload the furniture, jack up the wagon, and put in a new axle."

Joe turned to leave. Later, I wished I had let him, but I didn't. "Hey, where do you think you're going? We can use an extra pair of hands here."

He studied me a moment, an amused gleam in his

eyes. "You know better than that, old friend. I don't do no heavy lifting."

I nodded. "Well, Pard. You do now."

Believe or not, within an hour, we had fitted the new axle and tightened the lock nut down on the wheel. "Now, all we need is to load the furniture," I said.

Sunny jumped up in the bed. "You fellers hand me the table and chairs. I'll arrange them proper."

Joe, Twitch, and me grabbed the round table and hoisted it up to Sunny. Just as we managed to set it on the lip of the wagon bed, Twitch groaned. "Lord, this is heavy. I—watch out! I'm losing my grip."

The heavy table tilted to one side and crashed to the ground. The top popped away from the pedestal, and when the round pedestal slammed to the ground, gold coins poured from it.

Chapter Three

We all stood frozen in surprise, gaping at the pile of coins on the ground like we'd lost what few wits we had jangling around in that hollow spot where our brain was supposed to be.

"What the . . ." Twitch muttered.

"Would you look at that," Joe whispered, picking up a coin. "Gold double eagles. No wonder it was so heavy." He strained to set the pedestal upright and peered down the hole in the middle. He jammed his hand into the pedestal. "It's plumb full of gold coins." He glanced around at me. "Look at them. Double eagles." His voice quivered with excitement as he held up a handful of double eagles and let them trickle through his fingers back into the pedestal. "There must be a thousand of them," he whispered.

At that moment, the idea that Wilhelmina Madison had taken advantage of us outweighed my concern over the broken mirror. I looked up at Sunny. "I reckon this is why the lady wanted the wagon in a safe place."

With a wry gin, Sunny drawled, "Can't say I blame the lady."

For several seconds, maybe even a couple minutes, we all just stood and stared at the glittering coins. "Well, boys, we're getting nothing done just standing here," I said. "Let's put the thing back together."

Twitch and Joe scooped up the coins and dumped them back in the pedestal while I studied the decorative metal collar on the pedestal. Four metal latches protruded from the top of the collar. On the bottom of the tabletop was a matching collar, except it had four slots, designed to receive the latches. Concealed springs freed the latches.

"I heard about these old tables," I said. "Back before the war, plantation owners used them to hide their money." I glanced at Joe, but his shining eyes were fixed on the table. With a sinking feeling, I knew exactly what he was thinking.

Ten minutes later, we had everything loaded, even the broken mirror and its pieces. We snugged the tarp down over them.

Before we left the barn, I turned to them. "Look, boys. This is something we can't say nothing about. Word gets out, and every owlhoot in Kansas, Indian Territory, and North Texas will be after us." I looked directly at Joe. "How about riding back to Texas with us?"

He chuckled and reached for the almost empty bottle. "No thanks, Pard. I told you. Remember? I got business over in Fort Leavenworth." He hesitated. "Don't worry. Your secret is safe with me."

I watched him as he walked away, wondering if I could believe him.

I left Twitch with the wagon while I went back to the doctor's office, my initial irritation at Bill's deliberate secrecy waning. After all, she didn't know us from Adam.

She looked up when I entered the back room of the doctor's office. A tiny smile played over her lips. I nodded. "Everything is taken care of. The wagon's safe." Pausing a moment, I added, "I mean, *everything* is safe."

She frowned at the nuance in my tone. She looked into my eyes, as if to read what was behind them. I nodded slowly, and her eyes grew wide with apprehension.

"Don't worry," I said. "I told you, everything is safe. Twitch is there with the wagon."

I nodded to Timmy who was engrossed in a book, then to the door. She understood. Rising, she said, "Look after your sister for a few minutes, Timmy. She's sleeping. If she awakens, I'll be out on the boardwalk getting some fresh air."

He wrinkled his forehead in a frown. "What about me? I need some fresh air, too."

"Later," Bill said sweetly, but I caught a hard edge to her tone.

* * *

On the boardwalk, I looked down at her. "I think we deserve some kind of explanation. I couldn't figure why anyone put so much stock in furniture. It didn't make sense then. It does now."

She studied me for several moments, then hesitated as two women wearing bustles and carrying parasols passed. "I didn't know if I could trust you. I still don't, but now, I don't have a choice. You don't strike me as the kind who would kill me and steal my gold in front of two children. Of course, as far as I know, you might kill them too."

"Look, Lady. All I want to do is get back to Texas. I'm offering to help because I've known your uncle for years. He's a fine old man. I've got no interest in your gold. What puzzles me, though, is why you didn't send it through bank drafts instead of hauling it yourself. You could have half the outlaws in the country after you."

"The carpetbaggers, Mr. Morgan. Uncle Hewitt says they run all the banks, even the one he has used in Marion, Texas. He doesn't trust any bank. They want his ranch, and the way they raised his taxes, he'll lose it if I don't get this gold to him."

I understood what she was saying. Had J.R. Drennan not ratholed his money over the years, the carpetbaggers would have his place. Even the fourteen thousand dollars that was his share of the last cattle drive would only hold off the northern vermin another year or so.

"How much is there?"

She looked around to make sure no one would overhear. "Almost twenty-five thousand dollars," she whispered.

Well, once again, old Twitch had hit the target right in the bull's eye. When things start going wrong, they don't stop. Maybe that old man was smarter than I gave him credit for.

That night Twitch and I planned to stay in the barn, sleeping in the wagon, one at a time. "We can do that until we pull out," I announced.

"When is that?"

"Soon as the girl is able. Couple days."

"She seems like a good little girl, but that brother ain't worth shooting."

I had to agree. "Someone needs to jerk a knot in his tail. But, I can promise you one thing, by the time this trip is over, he won't be such a smart alec."

"What he needs is his back end worn out."

"And you're just the man who can do it, huh?" I grinned at him.

He ignored my question. He just yawned and stretched his lanky arms over his head. "Wish I had me a drink of tarantula juice." When he lay down I could sense the expectation in the air. "Yes, sir. Sure would help me to rest a heap better." I said nothing. A few minutes later, he muttered. "My bones ache something fierce." He shifted restlessly in the wagon bed. "Now, I'm getting me a crick in my neck."

Finally I spoke up. "You ain't never going to be quiet unless I go get you a bottle of whiskey, are you?"

Feigning injured pride, he replied, "Why, Clay.

How can you say such a thing? It's just that if I rest up good and proper, then there ain't much chance I could let you down on the trail."

It was my turn to playact. Feigning disgust, I rolled from my blankets and tugged my hat down on my head. "I can see the only way I'm going to get any sleep tonight is if I buy you that blasted bottle of whiskey."

I glared at Twitch who just gave me a pleasantly smug smile.

Later, leaning against the bar while the bartender filled the bottle from the kegs, I froze when I overhead the words "gold coins" mentioned. I glanced sidelong into the mirror behind the bar and spotted two of the hardcases Joe had spoken to the night before.

I paid for the whiskey and headed out of the bar, planning on running Joe down and peeling a large chunk of his hide from his worthless carcass.

We met just outside the batwing doors of the saloon. A large grin popped across his face. "Hey, Clay. Come on back in. I'm buying."

"You lying, no-good—" I charged him, jamming my forearm in this throat and slamming him up against the saloon. "Don't talk to me about drinks, you worthless barrel of shucks."

"What the—" He shoved me roughly away. "What's the matter with you?" Fire flashed in his eyes.

Lowering my voice, I growled. "You're not that dumb, Joe."

"Dumb? About what?"

I took a step toward him and stuck my nose in his

face. "The gold, that's what. The gold. You couldn't keep your mouth shut about the gold, could you?"

He shook his head emphatically. "I didn't say nothing. I ain't told no one. I gave you my word."

"Yeah, you did. And like a loco bull, I believed it."

Joe grinned easily. "What's going on, Pard? What put the burr under your saddle?"

I hooked my thumb in the direction of the bar. "I just overheard two of your business partners in there talking about gold coins. That's what's got into me." I squeezed the neck of the whiskey bottle until I thought it would break. Anger roared in my ears. For a moment, I truly considered breaking that full bottle of whiskey over his head.

He must have seen the malice in my eyes for he took a step aside and held up his hands. "Hey. No. Not me, Clay. I said nothing. I swear. On my mother's grave. I didn't tell no one what we saw in the barn this afternoon."

I eyed him suspiciously. "I saw how you looked at those coins. It was the same way I've seen you look at a lot of things that suddenly disappeared."

"Maybe so. Maybe that's right, but you're the one jasper in this world I wouldn't lie to, Clay. Sure, I'd like to have the gold, but I promised you." He held up his hands in surrender.

For several seconds I studied him. "You've played the innocent before."

He chuckled. "You mean like that time up in Denver? Sure, but not like that with you. I've always been straight with you. Give me one time when I ain't."

I pondered his question. Finally I grunted. "Okay, I can't." He grinned, and I added. "But just in case, I'm keeping an armed guard on that wagon all night. Any jasper comes snooping around will find himself mighty suddenly on the staircase down to hell."

Joe glanced at the Colt on my hip. "That Colt ought to tell you something about me, Pard."

"I reckon it should, but answer me this. What were those two hombres talking about if it wasn't the gold coins?"

"Got no idea." He shrugged. "I'm not saying they didn't say gold coins, but you've got to trust me that they weren't talking about . . ." He glanced around at the people passing us on the boardwalk. "About you know what," he added.

I wanted to believe Joe. He'd always done me right in the past. And while I didn't approve of some of the stunts he pulled, he had never taken advantage of me. I studied him a few more moments.

A crooked grin curled his lips. "Have I ever lied to you, Partner?"

Hesitantly, I replied. "No. I reckon not."

"Well, I'm not lying now."

I let out a long sigh. "All right. I suppose I just overreacted. Sorry, Joe."

He clapped his hand on my shoulder. "Hey, I would have done the same. Don't worry about it. Now, you sure I can't buy you a drink?"

"No." I held up the bottle. "Twitch is waiting for this one."

"Well, you take care. You'll be traveling through

some mighty dangerous country. Keep your eyes peeled, you hear?"

"Don't worry. I figure to maybe talk to some of those Indian lawmen into riding along with us. I'm not too worried about getting to Baxter Springs, but I don't cotton to crossing Indian Territory without some help. Once we hit Texas, we'll be all right."

He offered his hand. "Well, good luck, Pard."

"Thanks, Pard," I replied, shaking his hand.

Despite Joe's reassurance, I couldn't sleep much that night, worrying about Joe and his compadres. So, instead of sleeping, I wrote the letter I had promised J.R. I wasn't much on writing, but I included all the details, knowing that old rascal would have done the same thing as Twitch and me.

Next morning, Sunny stayed with the wagon while Twitch and I posted the letter for the next stage and then ordered a couple trays of hot breakfast and toted them over to the little back room.

Even Louisa nibbled on a buttered biscuit smothered with gravy despite Bill's warning for her not to over-load her stomach. While we were eating, the doctor looked in, checked Louisa, and nodded his satisfaction with her improvement. "If nothing goes wrong, she can leave in the morning."

Twitch, Sunny, and me spent the day rigging a can-vas bonnet for the wagon and stowing enough staples to get us to Baxter Springs.

Sunny frowned. "How far is Baxter Springs?"

"I figure we can make it in a week with no problems," I replied. "What do you think, Twitch?"

"Why don't we figure on a week and a half? Something's going to go wrong. I feel it in my bones."

I shook my head in frustration at the old man.

Twitch and I were perched on the opera rail of the corral at sunset when a group of riders ambled past. It was the hardcases we'd seen Joe hobnobbing with. They headed west out of town, taking the road to Ft. Leavenworth.

But Joe was not with them.

Their dust had not settled when I spotted Joe push through the batwing doors and head down the boardwalk toward the train station.

Twitch drawled. "Wonder why he ain't with them other line riders."

I wondered the same thing. "Beats me." I slid off the top rail. "Think I'll find out. You stay here with the wagon."

Joe walked past the train station to the docks on the Missouri River. Goods from riverboats were stacked high, waiting to be hauled into the warehouses. Joe paused by a stack of boxes near the edge of the pier. He was rolling a cigarette when I appeared.

He didn't seem all that surprised to see me. "Hello, Clay," he said as he touched a match to the cigarette. "Figured you'd be gone by now."

"Joe." I nodded in the direction of the hardcases. "Your friends left town."

With a shrug, he grunted. "Yeah. I decided I didn't care all that much for their company. I got a feeling those old boys are heading for trouble. They didn't much like it when I backed out, but they didn't have the guts to do nothing about it." He patted the six-gun on his hip.

His response pleased me. "So you're at loose ends, huh?"

"Reckon you could say that," he replied.

"Why don't you ride along with us, then? We can always use another gun."

"Maybe I just wi—" His eyes grew wide, and his hand flashed for his sixgun.

Behind me, a gun roared. Joe screamed and spun around, tumbling headlong into the muddy river.

I spun, just in time to see the muzzle of a revolver slam into my forehead.

Chapter Four

Somewhere in the distance, I heard voices, then I felt fingers touch the welt on my forehead. "Knot the size of a horse's apple. Bleeding like sin, but he'll live," a disconnected voice said.

"Who is he?" another asked.

"Don't know. I heard a shot and looked out the station window in time to see some jasper whop him in the head, then run off back to town."

By now, I was coming around enough to feel the sharp pain in my head, but was still too groggy to sort my thoughts. I yearned for the return of the painless bliss of unconsciousness.

A third voice interrupted. "What's going on here?"

The second voice explained. "I heard a shot. When I looked around, I saw some jasper crack this feller's skull, then run off."

A boot toe nudged my ribs, and a hard voice said. "You. Cowboy. What happened here?"

I managed to open my eyes and stare up at the fuzzy outline looking down at me. I blinked once or twice, trying to clear some of the cobwebs. Suddenly, I remembered Joe. "Joe!" I sat up abruptly, and my head exploded.

A strangled groan clawed its way from deep in my chest. I pressed my hands against my head as hard as I could, trying to still the excruciating pain. Slowly, it eased.

The sheriff demanded, "Who's Joe? Anybody here know?"

There was a chorus of muttered "no's."

"How about it, Cowboy? Who's Joe?"

"A friend," I muttered. "We was talking. Someone shot him. He fell in the river. When I looked around, I got cold-cocked."

"Take a look, Seth. See if there's a body down there."

Blood dribbled through my fingers and dripped onto my lap. I fought against the throbbing pain as I struggled to stand. Hands steadied me. I leaned against the wooden crates and peered across the river. By now, dusk had settled in, and all I saw in the river were a few bobbing logs.

The sheriff studied me suspiciously, waiting for me to speak. I spoke haltingly, "We—Joe and me—we were standing here talking. Joe saw someone behind me. Next I knew, he got shot, and when I turned around, someone hit me with the muzzle of a six-gun."

"You get a good look at him?"

I started to shake my head, but decided against it. "No. All I saw was the barrel just as it hit me."

The agent from the train station returned. "Been up and down the dock, Sheriff. No sign of a body. It might snag on the shore tonight."

The sheriff studied the broad river. "And it might not." He looked back at me. The skeptical look in his eyes told me he was not completely convinced that I had nothing to do with the shooting despite the knot on my head. He shucked my six-gun and smelled the muzzle. "What's your name, Cowboy? And what's your business here?"

Still somewhat addled by the blow, I brokenly detailed the purpose of my trip, and the explanation for the delay in our leaving Kansas City. "The girl and her brother are in the back room of the doctor's office with Bi—I mean, Miss Wilhelmina Madison. My partner, Twitch Mabry, is at the freight yard. One of the employees there, Sunny, is an old friend."

"Sunny?" The sheriff looked at Seth.

The station agent nodded. "He's the black bullwhacker Finas hired sometime back. He come here from Colorado where he said he was with a cattle drive."

"That was my drive. We came up from Beaver Tail Valley down in Angelina County, just below Nacogdoches, Texas."

He studied me a few more seconds. "Where you staying?"

"Me and my partner are sleeping in the freight barn with our wagon."

He handed me the six-gun. "All right, but don't leave town unless I say so."

"Don't worry," I muttered, staggering on my feet and finally holstering my revolver after two or three efforts.

"Seth. Help this old boy back to his wagon. Can't have nobody passing out in the middle of the street. Gives the town a bad name."

Twitch and Sunny took over when we reached the freight yard. They helped me into the wagon, and while Sunny closed the door, Twitch poured three or four stiff slugs of whiskey down my gullet. It burned like blazes when it hit my belly.

Then he clambered down, announcing he was going to get the doctor. While he was gone, Sunny, unaware Twitch had already given me some whiskey, promptly poured another three or four slugs down my throat.

That Old Orchard whiskey didn't do much to ease the throbbing in my head, but it sure helped me ignore it.

The doctor, with Bill on his heels, came in behind Twitch. First thing Doc did was pour another three or four slugs of whiskey down me, and then while he tended my head, the other three shot questions at me from every direction.

The whiskey had me flying high. Between their hundred questions and my mumbled responses, it was thirty minutes before I managed to tell the whole story.

When the doctor finished with me, he cautioned Sunny and Twitch not to let me sleep for any length of time. "No telling what the blow might have done to the inside of his head, not that any of you cowpokes have anything in there. Still, there's no sense in taking any chances."

Later, as I stared at the ceiling of the barn, my head had cleared enough that I felt both anger and anguish over Joe's death. Who could have killed him? Then I remember him saying those hardcases didn't like the idea of his pulling out. Maybe that was it. He knew their plans, and they wanted to make sure he didn't spoil their play.

The night was a long one. Every time I drifted off, Sunny or Twitch would wake me. I was exhausted the next morning, and secretly I hoped the sheriff would keep us in town.

But, he didn't.

Just after sun up, he came into the freight yard. "Well, Mister Morgan, you folks can pull out whenever you want. Your story holds up. What do you want us to do with that friend if we find the body?"

"What does your undertaker charge for a burial?"

"Get a nice one for a double eagle."

Twitch and I exchanged looks, each aware of the irony of the price of the funeral. I fished in my pockets and handed over twenty dollars. "Make it a nice one. If you don't find Joe, then buy something for the jail."

* * *

We pulled out at noon with Bill perched on the seat beside Sunny, the two youngsters in back, and Twitch and me astride our ponies on either side.

Bill had dressed herself and the children for the trail, which was another hint she was no tenderfoot. Louisa wore a plain blue calico dress, a bonnet, and ankle high shoes while Timmy wore new denim pants, a cotton shirt, a new hat, and brogans. Bill, to my surprise, had opted for men's clothes rather than a dress.

"Dresses just get in the way out here," she remarked when she saw me staring quizzically at her trousers.

I glanced at Twitch who ticked up one side of his lips in a lopsided grin.

As far as I could tell, we drew no unusual attention as we pulled out of town. The trail was easy heading south for passing cattle herds had trampled the grass. In the distance, beyond the broad swath beaten down by trailing cattle, grassy hills, covered with four-foot high Indian Grass in gaudy bloom, rolled before us like waves in the ocean as far as the eye could see. Hard to believe such a sight could hide danger, but a clever stalker could stay below the crest of the hills until he was right on top of us.

Once, when I looked back, I spotted a cloud of dust. The hair on the back of my neck bristled. Next time I looked, it had disappeared, but I still had the tingling on the back of my neck. I glanced at Twitch who was watching me. He nodded tersely.

Throughout the afternoon, much to my annoyance, we met some travelers. I would have much preferred seeing no one, not as long as we carried twenty-five thousand dollars. An hour before dark, we reached the Osage way station, a stopover for the Overland Stage Company.

"I'm tired," Timmy moaned. "Can't we stop here?"

Bill looked around at me expectantly.

After pushing beeves to Denver, Dodge, and Abilene over the years, I had picked up the knack of figuring out where trouble could come from. In studying the way station and surrounding corrals, I saw too many places where trouble could be hiding. I shook my head. "We'll move on a couple miles."

"But I'm tired," Timmy whined. "I want to stop."

I ignored him as we moved out. I kept my eyes moving. I had seen nothing suspicious, but I could not rid myself of the feeling that not all was right. It had taken me a few years and close scrapes to learn to pay attention to that nagging feeling.

A mile or so from the station, a lone rider approached us from the south. He pulled to the side as we drew near. He was covered with grease worse than a buffalo skinner, and he smelled bad enough to gag a dog on a gut wagon. He touched grimy fingers to the brim of his hat. "Howdy, folks."

We pulled up. I rode up to him while Twitch edged off to his left. "Howdy."

There was a long pause. His beady eyes quickly took in the wagon and our numbers. "Going far?"

I took an instant dislike to the jasper. "Far enough."

Grinning, he tried to make conversation. "Where you folks be heading?"

Keeping my eyes fixed on his, I replied, "South."

His grin faded. "Ain't very talkative, are you, Stranger?"

"Not very, Stranger."

His eyes grew hard. He cut his eyes to the wagon where he let them rest on Bill and the children longer than just a casual glance, then to Twitch. With a curt nod, he clicked his tongue and sent his pony up the trail toward the way station.

Twitch drew close. "Scavenger if I ever saw one."

I nodded. "Yep." I looked around at the waving grass on the hills surrounding us. "His compadres could be out there right now watching us."

With a grunt, Twitch drawled, "Not yet."

I looked at him. He was right.

Another mile down the road, we pulled off the trail and moved back among the rolling hills where we built a small fire and quickly cooked supper. Grub on the trail isn't fancy, but Sunny did whip up some gravy and bacon.

While the others ate, I perched on the crest of a hill, studying the vast prairie surrounding us as darkness settled over it like a gently descending blanket. The immensity of the American prairie is almost impossible to describe. It is an experience that must be lived rather than expressed. Overhead is a great bowl, stretching farther than the eye can see. The size is frightening to some, an intimate treasure to others.

Often I'd pause on a hill and stare across countless miles at a silent prairie, the grass gently swaying in a soft breeze, watching the vagrant zephyrs swaying the top of the grasses like the footprints of God strolling across His prairie. At those times, I felt a closeness with nature that told me somewhere there was a greater power than any of us, a power given many different names by many different cultures.

From below, I heard Timmy complaining about the food. That was no surprise. That boy was the complainest youngster I had ever seen. Louisa, on the other hand, was shoveling bacon and gravy into her mouth like it was the last meal before Texas.

Sometime later, Twitch relieved me. "See anything?"

I shook my head. "Nope." I rubbed the back of my neck. "But, I still got a feeling."

He studied the country around us silently. Finally, he replied. "Yep, me too."

Bill had managed to coax a few words from Louisa, who promptly clammed up when I came into camp. I spoke to the child. "How you feeling?"

She stared at the ground.

Bill whispered. "Go ahead, Sweetheart. Tell him. It's okay."

Timmy broke in. "She didn't like the food any better than I did. It wasn't fit for hogs."

I didn't lose my temper, but I did raise my voice when I snapped at him. "You ate didn't you, Boy?"

He frowned at me, uncertain just what I meant.

"Well, answer me. Did you eat?"

He glanced at Bill, puzzled, then nodded, "Yes."

"That means you're worse than a hog."

"Huh?"

"You heard me."

"That's not what I meant. I meant—"

I took a step toward him. "I know what you meant. Now you listen to me, Boy, and you listen good. You got a bad habit of thinking you're better than everyone else. I got news for you. You aren't, and the sooner you understand that little piece of information, the easier things will be on you. I'll get you down to your grandfather in one piece even if I have to take a strap to you everyday of the trip. We've all got problems. This trip itself is one big problem, so if you've got something to complain about, keep it to yourself. Otherwise, you're going to have me to deal with."

He took a step back, then sidled toward Bill. I don't reckon his folks had ever talked that hard to him, but out here, there was no time to be wasted on a whining baby.

Bill gave me a look filled with daggers.

I didn't care. I was jumpy as a flea in a hot skillet, and the last thing I wanted to listen to was a spoiled brat or a woman making excuses for him.

Chapter Five

Needless to say, there was no conversation around the fire while I ate. The three of them, Bill, Louisa, and Timmy just stared at me. Sunny was busy tending the horses.

After the meal, I sent the three to bed. "There's a pallet in the wagon. You can sleep there."

Timmy shook his head. "I don't sleep with girls. I—"

I glared at him and unbuckled my belt.

His eyes bugged out like a squashed frog. He gulped once, then clambered into the wagon. The firelight lit the faint grin on Sunny's face beyond the wagon.

After the three closed the pucker hole in the canvas bonnet, I squatted by the fire for an after supper cigarette. Sunny sauntered over to me. "Want me to relieve Twitch?"

I studied the darkness around us. "Might as well. I'll relieve you in a couple hours."

Twitch came in and poured a cup of coffee and rolled a cigarette. We sat beside the dying fire and spoke softly. In the distance a coyote wailed. "I got the feeling we might have us some visitors tonight, Clay," he muttered.

"I know so," I replied, studying the night.

"So, what do you have in mind?"

"The moon doesn't rise until late. They'll hit before that, so we'll give them a hand."

"Huh?" Twitch frowned, clearly puzzled. "What do you mean, we'll give them a hand?"

"Build the fire high. Pack the bedrolls so they look like we're sleeping. Then we'll each find us a spot in the shadows at the base of those hills."

"What if they suspect an ambush?"

"They won't, not after they spot the dummy bedrolls. They'll figure they caught us with our pants down."

"I hope you're right. I got a bad feeling something's going to go wrong."

"Well, stick that feeling under your hat and do what I say, you hear?"

Quickly, I briefed Bill of our plans. "When it starts, stay hunkered down. Keep the kids down."

Checking our Winchesters, we took our places in the darker spots around the camp. The thick grass was so tall that when a jasper lay down, he couldn't be seen from ten feet away.

I raised my head above the grass and peered at the fire. The flickering flames lit the bedrolls clearly.

Time dragged.

Overhead the stars slowly tracked their path across the heavens.

In the distance, a coyote howled. In another direction, a rabbit squealed, and then the heavy beat of wings told me an owl had just found its supper.

On the hill below which I lay, I heard a faint scratching. I peered into the bluish light cast by the stars, struggling to make out darker silhouettes in the night. I strained for any sound.

Then I heard a faint swishing sound. Denim against grass? A dark object appeared at the top of the hill to my right. I tried to make it out. Was it really there, or was it my imagination?

I decided to take no chances. Gingerly, I cocked the hammer of my Winchester and laid the front sight on the shadowy object. For all I knew, I might be staring at a bush, but I—

Suddenly, an orange flame erupted from the hilltop followed by the booming report of a rifle. Instantly, I began firing, pumping five shots at the shadow within three seconds. Behind me, the camp erupted in gunfire. Screams cut through the crack of the Winchesters and the boom of Spencers.

As quickly as it started, it was over. I waited, hammer cocked, for any additional gunplay. An eerie silence fell over the prairie.

From the wagon, Bill called out. "Is it over?"

"Stay down," I replied.

I crept to the top of the hill, pausing every few steps to crouch and listen. All I heard was the wind rustling the grass. I took another step and froze. Less than two feet in front of me lay a body. I held my breath, but there was no movement from the figure. I touched the muzzle to the motionless body. Still no movement.

Reluctant to take a chance he was feigning unconsciousness or death, I slammed the muzzle down on his chest. He didn't move.

I fumbled in the dark for his rifle and six-gun, after which I eased back down the hill to the small fire. Twitch and Sunny were waiting.

"I got mine," Sunny said.

"I got one of mine," Twitch said. "One got away. Disappeared into the night."

I muttered a soft curse.

"Can we come out now?" Bill's voice sounded from the wagon.

"Come on out." I turned to Sunny. "We best post lookouts. You go first. I'll spell you in a couple hours, and Twitch can finish out the night, but I don't reckon those waddies will come back."

Bill clambered down from the wagon and squatted by the fire. She had removed her bonnet, and her black hair cascaded over her shoulders. She looked from Twitch to me. I saw no trace of fear in her eyes. "Who were they?" The youngsters, wide-eyed, stayed closer to her than new bark on a tree.

"Scavengers. I figure that one of them was that old boy we met on the trail this afternoon."

"How did you know they would attack us?"

Twitch and me exchanged wry grins.

"What was that all about?" she asked. "Why were you two grinning at each other?"

"Nothing, really. How long you been back East, Ma'am?"

"Bill." She corrected me.

"Sorry. Habits are mighty hard to break—Bill."

"A long time," she replied to my question. "We lived in Fort Worth. My parents took me to Philadelphia when I was eight or nine."

"Well, after you're out here a spell, you'll learn that you figure anybody you don't know could be coming to take what you got."

She frowned. After a moment, she said. "In other words, you're suspicious of everyone you don't know."

Twitch nodded. "And sometimes of them that you do know, Ma'am." He gave me a warning look that told me he was referring to Joe Sterling.

"Most of the time," I said, "folks will surprise you because most of the time, they turn out to be decent and honest. But, you never trust strangers, not if you want to wake up the next morning."

Timmy glanced fearfully into the night around us and then scooted closer to Bill. She gestured to the darkness. "Will they be back?"

Twitch chuckled. "Three of them won't, but you can bet your bottom dollar there will be others. Maybe not from this bunch."

She looked up at me. "Were they after . . ." She hesitated and glanced at the wagon.

I shrugged. "Who can say? Scavengers will go after anything."

Bill studied me a moment, searching my face for reassurance that the scavengers were not after the gold. I grinned and nodded. "They probably figured they could sell the horses and wagon for a few dollars."

"Will there be more of them?"

Twitch spoke up. "Ma'am, where money is concerned, you can't keep word from leaking out any more than you can catch water with your fingers."

We moved out with the sun. The day promised to be clear and hot, but we were lucky enough to catch a gentle southerly breeze that danced over the Indian Grass. I never tired of watching the footsteps of the wind in the tall grass as it raced across the prairie. Occasionally, we crossed valleys of blue grama dotted with patches of purple tick clover, red and yellow Indian Blanket, and white Horse Nettles, a palette of color unmatched by human hand.

The day and night passed without incident. We met a handful of travelers, waved as the stage swept past on the way to Kansas City, and nooned with a couple wranglers from a Texas cattle drive.

I had paid little attention to the children, leaving them in Bill's hands. That night after the children went to bed, Sunny and I were quietly discussing the coming day's travel when Bill came to sit on the wagon tongue near the fire. I offered her some coffee, which she accepted.

"The children are exhausted," she said, glancing at the wagon.

"They'll get used to it. How about you?"

She arched an eyebrow and gave me a wry grin. "Me too. I've bounced around in buggies and hacks, but never in anything as rough as that wagon."

Sunny chuckled. "An old man up in Illinois once told me that every time he went to town, his Missus plopped a bucket of fresh milk in the back of his wagon. The wagon was so rough that by the time he got back home, he had him a bucket of churned butter."

Bill looked at him in disbelief. She glanced at me.

I shrugged and grinned. "Wouldn't surprise me."

"Well," she replied. "that's something I have to see to believe."

We all laughed.

When we moved out next morning, a sense of foreboding lay on my shoulders. Around noon, we hit the Cygnes River at Potter's Ferry. The ferry was a barge hooked to a rope stretched across the river that had once been one of the main highways into the West in the early settlement of the country. A thick, square beam was set in the port side stern and another in the port side bow. The draw rope had been strung through a hole near the top of each.

Willow and elm grew along the banks of the river. On a small rise several yards from the shore sat a ramshackle house grayed by the weather. It's four walls leaned in four different directions, and for the life of me, I had no idea what kept it standing other than the fact it was so dirty.

On the porch, a bearded hombre slouched in a rocking chair, eyeing us suspiciously as we drew close. I studied the house and the grounds around it, looking for any sign of others being about.

I nodded. "Howdy."

"Howdy." He didn't move. He just stared at us like we were bugs he planned to stomp under his foot.

"What's the charge for us and the wagon?"

He pursed his lips. "Wagons is two dollars, horses one, people two-bits."

I fumbled in my vest, extracted the money, rode up to the porch, and handed it to him. "Nine-fifty. Let's go."

He stretched his arm to take the money. For the first time, his eyes slid away from us, then quickly came back. He took the money. "Can't. Not yet."

"Why not?" I backed my pony from the porch and glanced warily at the stand of willow and elm stretching up and down the shoreline.

"Got some others coming. Figure on just one trip." He massaged his right shoulder. "Got the arthritis bad."

A crooked grin twisted my lips. "Didn't look that way when you took the money."

His eyes grew hard. "What do you mean by that, Stranger?"

"Just this." I shucked my six-gun and held it centered on his chest. "You're taking us across now. We're not waiting for anyone, you hear?"

"You're asking for bad trouble, Cowboy." He glanced toward the road we had just traveled.

The premonition earlier that morning burst into full bloom. "Maybe so, but you won't be here to see it if you don't light a shuck over to that ferry." I cocked my revolver. "Now."

Quickly, we loaded the wagon on the barge and lashed it down, then tied our ponies to the side rails. "Go," I shouted to the ferryman. He pulled, and we eased out into the river, which appeared to be about two hundred yards wide at this point.

At that moment, the pounding of hooves sounded from the road beyond the shack. The ferryman shot me a wild-eyed look, then dived overboard.

I shouted to Twitch and Sunny. "Pull." I grabbed my Winchester and knelt behind the large stern beam through which the draw rope was strung.

Half-a-dozen riders slid up to the shore just as the ferryman stumbled from the water. He turned and jabbed a finger toward us.

That's when I started firing, placing my first shots in the mud at their horses' feet. The frightened animals reared and twisted when the mud exploded and splattered into them. Two of the riders rolled off the back of their ponies. The others finally calmed theirs, and shucked their six-guns.

Slowly, the distance between the shore and us widened to fifty yards. At that distance, I wasn't worried about the accuracy of a handgun, but I was concerned about a lucky shot. "Stay down," I shouted to Bill and the children as I continued to rake the shoreline with .44 caliber slugs.

Suddenly, one of the hardcases darted through the trees to the rope and frantically slashed at it.

"He's cutting the rope," Twitch shouted. "The current will push us back to shore."

"That's what they think," I shouted above the roar of my Winchester.

Sunny looked around at me, the sweat on his face shining like diamonds. "Hope you knows what you're doing."

"Don't worry none about me. Just you keep pulling on that rope." I leaned my rifle against a rear wheel and pulled out my knife and stood behind the stern beam. "When he cuts that end, I'll cut the rope here. Then we'll wrap this end around your beam."

Twitch frowned, but Sunny grinned. "Yeah, and the current will swing us into the other bank."

Twitch's face lit in understanding. "Sounds logical, but do you think it'll work? You know what kind of luck you and me have."

I glanced up at Bill who was looking down from the front of the wagon. "It'll work."

We were in the middle of the river when the rope parted on the bank. In five or six quick slashes, I cut the rope at the ferry, which Twitch and Sunny then twisted around the stern beam several times.

The rope stretched tight, vibrating the water from it like a dog shakes himself. Propelled by the current, the ferry began a slow swing like a pendulum toward the far shore.

Bill shouted. "Clay! The scavengers! They're swimming the river!"

Chapter Six

I stared in disbelief at the riders swimming the river. I suspected that if you drilled a hole in every single one of their heads, you wouldn't find enough brains to grease a skillet.

Twitch came to stand beside me, Winchester in hand. "This somehow don't seem fair, Clay. Why, them jaspers are perched out there like whiskey bottles on a fence rail."

"Reckon he's right," Sunny said, clacking a shell in the chamber of his rifle.

"You bet he's right, but give those old boys the smallest chance, and you won't see any fair play from them." I jammed the butt of my rifle into my shoulder, and promptly slammed a lead plum into the shoulder of the nearest cowpoke. He screamed and tumbled from his horse.

Sunny and Twitch fired, and two more cowpokes

took a swim. The other three pulled up, staring at us uncertainly. When I threw my rifle to my shoulder again, they turned tail for the far shore.

Within minutes, the ferry scraped against the shoreline. The only problem was that the starboard side of the ferry instead of the bow had slid ashore.

We had to disembark the horses and rig up a harness to turn the ferry's bow into the shore so we could unload the wagon. In less than an hour, we had managed the task and had taken up our journey once again.

As we ambled down the road, a subdued voice from the wagon broke the rattle of the trace chains and the squeak of leather. "Mr. Morgan?"

I looked around. It was Timmy. His face was pale. "Do—Do we have any more rivers to cross?"

Bill gave me a pleading look. I didn't know what she meant exactly. "In a couple days. The Little Osage." His eyes grew wide, and I quickly added. "But we can drive across it."

A look of relief covered his face. "Good." He hesitated. "Louisa was scared," he added.

I suppressed a grin. Louisa wasn't the only one scared. "Well, Boy, tell her that the Little Osage is just like wading a creek."

He nodded and ducked back inside the wagon. Bill smiled at me.

I hadn't lied. The river might not be exactly like crossing a creek, but the spot I had in mind was between two and three feet deep. Naturally, when the rains filled the river's watershed, the water level rose, but there had been little rain the last few months so I wasn't too concerned.

I should have been, and I should have remembered Twitch's warning that "if something could go wrong, it will."

During the night, the prevailing winds shifted from the south to the east, which meant the warm air of the prairie was being pushed into the colder air of the Rocky Mountains to the west.

"Might have us some weather today," Twitch said, studying the sky as we moved out after breakfast.

"Hope not, at least until we cross the Little Osage."

Back to the west, faint clouds sat on the horizon. I had planned to camp on the north bank of the river tonight and cross in the morning, but the clouds building in the west worried me.

"Step the team up, Sunny," I said after pulling up beside the wagon. "I'd like to get across the river tonight."

Bill, on the seat beside Sunny, looked up at the brittle blue sky, clear of clouds except for those low-lying back to the west. "Anything wrong?"

"Can't tell for sure." I gestured to the western horizon. "Might be some weather over there. I'd feel a heap more comfortable if we made it across the river before it gets here. These creeks and rivers around here rise mighty fast."

She glanced over her shoulder in the direction of the children.

Slowly, but inexorably, the clouds rolled toward us,

great, billowing thunderheads probing the heavens with their dark crowns. Streaks of lightning zigzagged through the towering clouds.

We picked up the pace.

Twitch pulled up beside me and shifted his chaw of tobacco into his cheek. "If we're where I think we are on the trail, Clay, I figure the rain's going to beat us to the river."

I nodded, casting a worried looked at the approaching weather. I shivered. The worst spot a jasper can find himself in when such a storm is coming is out in the middle of the prairie where he is usually the tallest object around, a perfect target for lightning.

By now, the booming drums of thunder rolled across the prairie, still miles away, but heading our way with ominous deliberation.

Her eyes reflecting her concern, Bill looked at me. "Will it be bad?"

"Ain't none of them good out here, Ma'am," Sunny replied.

I nodded. "He's right, Bill. They're all bad out here."

We were still an hour from the Little Osage when the storm hit like a passel of starving cowpokes storming the chuck house. The wind switched abruptly, and a blast of cold air swept over us, whipping up the sand and stinging our skin.

Timmy had stuck his head out the pucker hole, but Bill motioned for him to go back inside. She tightened the hole.

To the west, a wall of rain rushed toward us, accompanied by streaks of lightning lancing the ground. Quickly, we all donned our slickers, preparing for the onslaught. Sunny had his hands full with the horses, which, frightened by the lightning and thunder, tugged wild-eyed at the reins. The nigh-leader, a heavy gray, reared and pawed at the air.

And then the rain hit, a heavy, drenching rain, the gusts of which rocked the wagon. Louisa screamed. I looked back to see Bill climbing through the pucker hole into the bonnet. I was mighty glad she was back there to calm the children.

Though it was only mid-afternoon, I could only see a few feet in front of me. I tugged my John B. down over my head and peered from under the brim. Luckily the road was worn enough so we had no trouble following it.

Lightning crashed about us. Desperately, I searched for shelter, knowing that none was about. I lay low on my pony's neck. Sunny had climbed back into the bonnet and was driving the team through the pucker hole.

Through the wall of rain, I spotted trees ahead. The Little Osage. I pulled up and motioned Twitch back to the wagon. Sunny stuck his head out, and I laid down my plan. "I'm going ahead to see how deep the water is. If we can make it, Twitch and me will tie ropes on to the wagon, and we'll drive right through the water. Understand?"

They both nodded.

I reined around and headed into the river. The water

had risen a foot or so to the belly of my pony. That would put a few inches of water in the bed, so I had Bill and the children stack blankets and pallets on the furniture to escape the water.

Rain lashed my face, drove into my eyes as I tied my rope around the axle next to the wheel. Twitch did the same on the opposite side. I looked around at Sunny and shouted. "Move 'em out, nice and steady."

My pony jiggered about when he stepped into the river, but I kept a tight rein and a soft voice. "That's it, boy. Steady there. Steady there."

The river was less than fifty yards wide at this point. On the far side, the shore rose to a knoll well away from the river. That's where we'd spend the night. If we succeeded in making it across the river, I reminded myself.

Halfway across, a loud roar sounded from upriver. Twitch looked around at me in alarm. Sunny heard it too, for he jumped back on the wagon seat and popped the reins on the rumps of his team. I dug my heels into my pony's flank. We had no time to waste. Within minutes, maybe even seconds, a wall of water would carom around the bend and carry away anything its path.

I urged my pony forward. "Come on, boy. Pull. Pull for all your worthless hide." Lightning struck into a tree downriver, bursting it into flames.

Slowly, the far bank grew closer. The roar upriver intensified. I tried not to think about it, desperately driving my struggling little cayuse toward the bank in a frantic effort to drag the wagon from the river before the wall of cascading water struck.

More than once, I'd witnessed unfortunate souls caught by a wall of water and swept away, screaming at the top of their lungs for help that could never come in time.

"Faster," I shouted at Twitch and Sunny. "Faster."

Finally, we reached shore. Twitch and Sunny reined up, but I shouted and waved for them to keep moving. "Not here. Up on that knoll yonder. We've got to reach that knoll."

The wagon wheels sank in the mud. We couldn't budge it. The roar of the oncoming flood grew louder. "Let's do it," I shouted into the raging wind and rain. The horses threw their chests into the harness. Their muscles bunched, then quivered with the strain. For what seemed like hours, we strained against the clinging mud. Slowly, we eased forward, one foot, then five, and then another five. The roar of the flood was deafening now, and before we moved another ten feet, the wall of water hit, one side smashing into the rear of the wagon and slamming it around. From inside came screams. Somehow, Sunny kept the team moving forward, jerking the wagon after them.

Finally, we reached the top of the knoll and sat silently on our horses, staring at the churning water below. Exhausted, Sunny sat slump-shouldered on the seat, the rain beating down on him, sluicing off his slouch hat. He looked down at me, his face drawn. It might have even been pale like Twitch's, but I couldn't tell. "I'm mighty glad you made us keep going. I don't suspect I could have handled that wagon if the water had hit us straight on," he muttered.

Lightning exploded with a sudden boom followed by a deafening crack. A large elm erupted in flames.

Suddenly, a green light played over the ears of Twitch's pony, startling the animal so that he swallowed his head and started pitching. Moments later, the light raced over Twitch as he clung to the wildly spinning horse.

Within moments, the green fire covered us all, horses, men, and wagon. Finally, Twitch managed to settle his pony down.

While I had witnessed the phenomenon before, it was still unnerving. The first time I saw it was with a herd of cattle during an electrical storm when the green fire leapt from horn to horn on the cattle, never harming any, until just as quickly as it had come, it vanished.

When I looked around, Bill and the children were staring goggle-eyed from the pucker hole at the display of fox-fire.

And as before, one instant it was there, the next, it had vanished.

The lightning moved past, but the rain continued, a steady fall. We rigged a canvas fly from one side of the bonnet to nearby trees. While Sunny put together a fire using some of the limbs from the lightning struck elm, Twitch and I added two sides to the fly, creating a snug shelter from the rain.

With a cheery fire blazing just inside the shelter, we

were soon warm and cozy, especially after we put ourselves around the pork stew Sunny had whipped together. That and steaming six-shooter coffee was about all a jasper could ask for.

Out of deference to Bill and the children, we dragged a dead log under the fly so they'd have something to sit on. We just squatted, a position I always found right comfortable.

Louisa still wasn't talking, but she had an appetite. Timmy even ate without complaining though from time to time, he shot me a surly look. Come to think of it, I hadn't heard him complain since I threatened to wear out the seat of his britches.

I don't remember my own Pa, but J.R. Drennan, the old man who raised me from the time I was no bigger than a flea, was a great believer in applying leather to the seat of a surly child. I learned that lesson early on.

The one advantage of the storm was that even the scavengers would be sheltering up. Still, I reckoned we'd be smart if we continued to take shifts tonight.

Bill stared into the fire, her hair falling about her slender shoulders. She was a right handsome woman. Pretty in fact. She looked around at me, then smiled at the children beside her. "So Timmy and Louisa will be on the ranch next to my uncle and me."

I nodded. "Yep."

"How did you happen to get the job of picking up the children?" She hastily added. "If you don't mind my asking."

"Don't mind. J.R., that's their granddaddy, asked me to pick them up, so I did."

She frowned. "Just like that? You work for him? Is that it?"

Twitch chuckled. "Work for him. Why, Ma'am, old Clay here don't do nothing but work for old J.R. I swear that old man is a mighty hard taskmaster."

I shot Twitch a dirty look, then glanced at the children who were hanging on to every word we uttered. "You know better than that. He's a fine old man. I'd do anything I could for him."

My crusty old partner laughed. "Just joshing." He turned to Bill. "Them two think the other hung the moon. I ain't never seen nothing like it. If old J.R. asked Clay here to take on a hundred Comanche with only a knife, he'd do it."

Timmy and Louisa looked at each other, puzzled.

"You're exaggerating again, Twitch. You know better than that."

With a tiny frown on her forehead, Bill asked, "Is he some kin to you?"

"No. Not really. He found me wandering about on the prairie when I this high," I said, holding my hand about three feet above the ground. "I don't remember much. He told me later that when he questioned me about how I had come to be out there all by myself, I couldn't remember. Never have," I said with an indifferent shrug.

She nodded. "Then how did you come to have a last name different than his?"

I studied the coffee in my cup. I was always uncomfortable talking about my past for it reminded me that a part of me, although not much, but a part of me was missing. "The name had been pinned to my shirt. J.R. figured that since back then there were orphan trains bringing orphans from the East to folks out here, I might have been with a wagonload of orphans, and we got jumped by Comanche or Apache." I sipped my coffee.

Twitch snorted. "Tell her the rest." I looked around at him, but before I could reply, he said. "Old J.R. raised Clay here like a son. Why, he even up and adopted him one time when the circuit judge come through."

Bill leaned back and nodded. "Now I understand. He's your father."

Nodding slowly, I replied, "The only one I ever knew."

She glanced at the children by her side. A warm smile played over her lips. "And these two are your niece and nephew. You're their uncle."

I had not even considered the youngsters were my kin, but I supposed Bill was right. I considered that likelihood for a few moments. I reckoned it would be right pleasant to have some family around.

Timmy jumped up, spilling his plate of stew to the ground. His face turned red, and he screamed. "No! No! You're not my uncle. We don't have an uncle. Mother told me so. You're lying." He spun and scrabbled up into the wagon.

The boy's reaction took me by surprise, but before I could say a word, Louisa stared at me in wonder. "Are you really my uncle?"

I was so surprised that she had spoken, I couldn't answer. All I did was nod.

Chapter Seven

Bill walked up as I was saddling my pony the next morning. She held her sunbonnet in her hand, and her shiny black hair fell about her shoulders. She was a handsome woman, mighty handsome. She looked up at me. "How did you sleep last night?"

Puzzled, I frowned. "Fine. Like always. Why?"

She shrugged. "I don't know. I thought that maybe Timmy's outburst might have upset you."

My frown deepened. "Upset me? Why would the tantrum of a spoiled boy upset me?"

Bill glanced at the ground, obviously uncomfortable. "It's just that, well, he cried off and on all night. I figured that maybe since he is your nephew, you might want to mend some fences."

I studied her a few moments, wondering if she was just pulling my leg. She couldn't be serious. I jerked the cinch tight around my horse's belly. The animal shied, and angrily I jerked it tight again and buckled it snugly. "He might be my nephew, but I got no fences to mend with him."

"You mean, it doesn't bother you the way he feels about you? That he refuses to believe you're his uncle?" There was a trace of disbelief in her voice.

"No, Ma'am. I got more concern about swatting a horsefly than what that whining brat thinks."

She knit her brows. "But he's just a boy."

I swung into the saddle. "A boy that had better grow up."

"But—"

Holding tight to my temper, I interrupted. "Listen, Bill. I reckon you got good intentions, but go practice them on someone else. Not me. I got work enough to do getting us down to Texas."

She jammed her fists in her hips. "Why, why you insensitive . . ." She stammered for words, but they didn't come. With a sharp cry of anger, she spun on her heel and stomped back to the wagon.

At that moment, Louisa stuck her head through the pucker hole. When she saw me, she gave me a shy smile and a brief wave.

I waved back. Things were getting complicated.

We traveled the next few days without incident. I was beginning to relax. Apparently, Joe Sterling had told me the truth. He had kept our secret, or we'd still be fighting off scavengers and various other owlhoots. I cringed when I thought about Joe. I sure missed him. But, he should have known better. The kind of fourflushers he was running with couldn't be trusted. Unfortunately, Joe learned that lesson the hard way.

While on one hand, I could relax about the gold, on the other, I was fighting the icy silence of Bill. She'd been colder to me than the ice Frank Barlow used to chill his beer back in his saloon in Marion, Texas.

In truth, I tried to see her point, but it always came back to the fact that she thought I should kowtow to a spoiled child.

I couldn't help grinning when I thought about how old J.R. would jerk a knot in the boy's tail. If Bill thought I was insensitive, just wait till she got a taste of J.R's sensitivity level.

Eight days after leaving Kansas City, we spotted Baxter Springs, near the border of Indian Territory.

"About time," Sunny said, when I pointed out Baxter Springs. "We be running mighty shy of grub."

"Reckon we'll lay over a day or so. Repair the rig. Rest up. We'll camp outside Fort Blair."

"Clay! Look!" Sunny pointed to a small herd of deer grazing on the side of a nearby hill. "Fresh meat," he said, reining up and fitting the butt of his Winchester in his shoulder.

I held my breath as he squeezed off a shot.

The deer looked up and stared at us, seemingly unperturbed.

"Some shot you are," I whispered.

Sunny frowned. "I don't figure how that happened. I was sure that I hit that one on the outside. Why—"

At that moment, the deer Sunny had pointed out crumpled to the ground.

Sunny laughed. "What was that you say, Boy? Why, I shot him so good, he didn't know he was dead."

I held up a hand and grinned sheepishly. "I reckon I owe you an apology."

"And I sure be going to take it."

Twitch rode up. "Well, Boys, I hate to tell you, but that venison is going to go bad if you two don't stop palavering."

He was right. Quickly we dressed the deer and tossed it in the back of the wagon.

Just before we reached the fort, the off-leader began to limp.

Twitch shook his head. "See there, Clay. I knew something was going to happen."

Baxter Springs was a wide-open cowtown, an anything goes stop-off for cattle drives heading for Kansas City. It sported a main street lined with a motley assortment of buildings of clapboard, canvas, and sod.

Drovers would leave their herds to fatten up on the luxuriant grasses of Indian Territory while they rode into town to visit the saloons and the other attractions. From noon to early morning, gunfire, laughter, music, and shouts filled the air. The only reason late mornings were quiet was that all the revelers were sleeping off the night before while the storeowners were making ready for the coming day.

I didn't figure many of the drovers would go anywhere near the fort, so that was the reason I picked such a location for our camp.

Even before Sunny unhitched the team, he checked

the off-leader's hooves. Holding the front hoof between his knees, he pulled his knife and dug under the
shoe. "A rock," he announced without looking up.
"Looks like a bruise on the frog too." He lowered the
foot. "It'll be fine with a little rest."

The children stayed closer than two coats of paint
to Bill that first morning when she went into town.
Twitch stared after the three as they reached the out-
skirts of Baxter Springs. "Reckon they'll be okay?"

"Yep. It's early. Most of those cowpokes are sleeping off last night's tarantula juice. Be noon before the
excitement starts up again."

We made the most of the day, greasing the wheels,
stocking up on grub for the five-day journey to Muskogee down in the middle of Indian Territory. Sunny
tended his team like a Mama cat, rubbing them down,
massaging their legs, watching their intake of food and
water.

Around dusk that first night, we all gathered around
the campfire except Timmy, who remained sulking in
the wagon. Several times, Bill shot me baleful looks,
but I ignored them.

The succulent aroma of Sunny's cooking assailed our
nostrils as well as those of three homesick soldiers who
wandered into our camp yearning for grub other than
that the army provided. We invited them to supper, and
Sunny earned himself a reputation by frying up thick
venison steaks, a skillet of corn mush, hot sourdough
biscuits straight from the spider, and a mock apple pie.

We slept the sleep of the dead that night.

*   *   *

Next morning at breakfast, Bill glanced up at me over her cup as she sipped her coffee. "Thought you might like to know that Timmy feels bad about the other night."

I studied her a moment. "He say that?"

She nodded, sipping her coffee.

After considering her information, I grunted. "Good. Maybe he's growing up some."

Her eyes turned chilly, and the muscles in her jaws writhed like snakes. "You're not going to say anything to him?"

"Nope."

"Why not?" Her question was testy.

With a shrug, I replied, "I just want to see if he's just airing his lungs."

She frowned. "Airing his lungs?"

"Yep. Just talking, not doing."

Her eyes drilled into mine. "You—You're impossible."

I grinned. "No, Ma'am. I'm not."

For the first time, she didn't remind me to call her Bill instead of Ma'am.

Later, while Bill and Louisa gathered elderberries from along a nearby stream, we put the finishing touches on the wagon and the gear, cleaned our rifles and handguns, checked for sufficient cartridges, spitted some venison to smoke, and then generally whiled away the day, even to the luxury of a short nap in the afternoon.

A toe nudging me in the side jerked me from my nap. I looked up at Twitch who nodded toward town. "Company," was all he said.

I sat up and blinked against the bright sunshine outside the canvas fly that provided our shade. I squinted at the two figures crossing the small patch of prairie between our camp and the small village. I made out a cowpoke dragging a boy after him. I pushed myself to my feet, curious.

Then I heard a familiar voice boom across the prairie. "Clay! Clay Morgan!"

The broad brim of his hat shaded the cowboy's face, but as soon as I heard the voice and connected it with those broad shoulders, I knew who he was. Rafe Abernathy, a trail mate of mine on a couple cattle drives.

"Would you look at that," Twitch exclaimed, stepping out from under the canvas fly.

Rafe was dragging Timmy after him. The young boy was screaming fiercely and struggling to break free of the cowboy's steel grip.

Bill and Louisa came around from the rear of the wagon where they had been mixing up some elderberry cobbler for the evening supper. "What on earth!" she exclaimed.

The mischievous grin on Rafe's rugged face was as wide as the Missouri River. He stopped a few feet from the small fire, his legs spread wide, and his grin growing even wider. Timmy twisted and jerked in an effort to escape Rafe's grasp, but the large cowboy held the struggling boy with as little effort as he would a rabbit.

"Clay! You old son-of-a-gun. What are you doing out here?"

I glanced at Timmy, then back to Clay. "I reckon I could ask you the same thing. Who do have there?"

"Huh?" He looked down at Timmy. "Oh, you mean this little rabbit? Well, now, Clay. There's a story behind this—a right interesting little story."

Timmy jerked back, but Rafe's fingers sunk in the boy's shoulder. The boy winced, cut his eyes toward Bill, then cried out, "Ouch. That hurts."

Rafe looked back to me, but spoke to Timmy. "Then best you stop fighting it, Son. You're stuck on the end of my arm like bees on honey until I turn you loose." He glanced at Bill, then he spoke to me. "You married now, Clay?"

Twitch chuckled. My ears burned. I didn't dare look at Bill. "No. Just helping get the wagon and passengers back to Texas."

"So this one," he said, jerking Timmy forward until the boy was facing me from five or six feet. Timmy stared at the ground. "This one ain't yours, huh?"

"He's my nephew, more or less."

Rafe shoved his battered gray hat to the back of his head revealing dark eyes that glittered with laughter. "Well, if I was you, I'd burn this button's behind until he couldn't sit down. Or, maybe that's what you already done that caused him to come in to town and try to hire someone to plow up the ground with you."

Behind me, Bill gasped. Twitch guffawed, but stifled it when I shot him a hard look.

I looked at Timmy who stared back at me with a defiant look on his face.

The grin remained on Rafe's bearded face. He gave Timmy a shove toward me. As soon as the boy felt the fingers release his shoulder, he scampered up into the wagon.

For several moments, Rafe and me stared at each other. "Are you pulling my leg, Rafe? It ain't funny if you are."

He shook his head and pulled a pint of whiskey from his back pocket and tossed it to me. "Gospel truth, Clay. Good thing he didn't get to some of those likkered up cowpokes. They's a bunch of them just drunk enough to take him up on it."

All I could do was shake my head, so I did. Then I took a long pull on the pint and shook my head again.

Chapter Eight

Rafe was in a talking mood, and not having run across me in four or five years, I obliged him. We strolled out across the prairie aimlessly, rolling our Bull Durhams, nipping at the bottle, and filling in the years for each other.

"I joined this drive in Dallas," he said. "Only trouble we run across come from some young bucks down in the territory. Choctaw, a few Comanche. A mixture of them young ones that still got a mad on at the world." He hooked his thumb over his shoulder. "What are you hauling?"

"Furniture and folks. The woman's a school teacher. The boy, and his sister, are J.R.'s grandchildren."

"J.R.?"

"You remember. The old man that adopted me."

His eyes lit with understanding. "You think that's why the youngster don't cotton to you? He figures

78

you're some kind of competition for him with the old man?"

I shrugged. "I got no idea, Rafe. Truth is, I never even thought about that. I reckoned he was angry over his ma and pa getting themselves killed. I knew he didn't like me, but I never figured he'd go far enough to want to see me plowed under."

Rafe chuckled and took another drink. "He's just a kid."

"You say he wanted to hire you, huh? What was he going to use for money?"

He fished in his pocket and dug out a gold coin. "You ain't going to believe it, but with this double eagle. A twenty dollar gold piece."

Well, sir, I felt like someone had hit me between the eyes with a singletree.

Rafe saw the dazed expression on my face. "You all right, Clay? What's wrong?"

"Huh?" I shook my head. "Oh, nothing, nothing. A double eagle you say?"

"Yep. Purtiest little gold coin you ever seen." He flipped it up in the air to me.

The double eagle landed in the palm of my hand. I stared at it for several seconds.

He chuckled. "Sort of a puzzle, huh? Makes a jasper wonder what to do about it." He stared at the wagon. "You remember that drive we made from San Antone to Abilene?"

I looked up from the coin. "I reckon that's one I won't forget. Just like old Twitch says, everything that could go wrong, did."

Rafe shook his head. "I'll never forget that contrary steer that kept trying to take over the lead from Old Satan."

With a grin, I nodded. "Old Satan was mighty proud of leading the herd, and he wasn't about to let that steer take over. It was a sight," I added, laughing softly.

"We can laugh now, but we sure weren't laughing when old Satan tore into that steer," Rafe drawled.

"Old Cookie threw a hissy fit when the two bovines slammed into his chuck wagon."

"Yep. Well, Old Satan sure enough handed that hard-headed steer a good licking." He paused, took a nip from the bottle and passed it to me, then stopped and stared back at the wagon. "That steer never tried to take Old Satan's place again."

I studied the wagon for several seconds. "Could be you're right."

"Could be." I dropped the double eagle in my vest pocket.

We headed back to the wagon, finishing off the pint between us on the way back. "When are you old boys pulling out, Rafe?"

"In the morning. What's the trail like up to Kansas City?"

"A few scavengers. The Little Osage flooded, but likely it'll be down by the time you reach it."

"Well, you folks get your eyes peeled. Like I said, there's a few bands of young bucks roaming the territory." He grinned crookedly and took my hand.

"Been good seeing you again, Clay. Let's don't us let another four or five years pass by."

"You know where I am down in Angelina County, Texas, Rafe. I got a spot for you anytime you want it."

"Thanks," A wry grin played across his face, "and look out for that young steer."

I watched Rafe stroll back down to the nearest saloon. A part of me felt a sense of sadness that I wasn't with him. He was a good man, rough as a cob about the edges, but one no hombre would be ashamed to ride the river with. You hate to part with old friends like that, but then, everyone has his own direction, and mine was south.

Pausing to watch Louisa and Bill mixing up the cobbler, I wondered if I should tell them about the marauding Indians. I decided to keep quiet. What they didn't know wouldn't hurt them.

I hoped.

Glancing at the wagon, I considered what to do about Timmy. I pulled out the double eagle and stared at it. I wasn't much of a hand with children, but I knew he must be full of rattlesnake venom to pull such a stunt. I decided to say nothing of the incident, not even of the double eagle. In all fairness to him, it might have belonged to him. I slipped it in my pocket. If it did, I'd give it back to him.

Tension about the camp that night was thicker than flies on a watermelon. Bill insisted Timmy join us for supper. I supposed she figured that by forcing the two of us together somehow we would suddenly, miraculously patch up our differences. I reckon she was a very sincere woman, but I didn't figure she could tell skunks from housecats when it came to solving problems between kin.

Timmy kept his eyes lowered, refusing to look at me. I ignored him, content to put myself around venison, hot biscuits, cream gravy, and two bowls of elderberry cobbler. To my surprise as I finished the second bowl, Louisa scooted next to me. "Timmy said you aren't my uncle."

I looked down at her, then cut my eyes to Timmy. He stared deliberately at the food in his plate. "Well, child, in a way, he's right. Your grandfather found me when I was younger than you." Briefly, I told her my story, about the adoption, about how he was the only father I could remember. "So, I'm not blood kin like you and your brother, but I am legally his son. Now, if you want me to be your uncle, I reckon I'd be pleased. But if you don't, I won't think nothing bad about you."

She studied me a moment, then nodded. "I'd like for you to be my uncle."

A warm smile played over Bill's lips, and a small lump formed in my throat.

After the children were in bed, Bill approached the campfire. I could feel the coolness in her manner. "What are you going to do to Timmy?"

Sunny and Twitch cut their eyes toward me.

"Nothing," I replied, sipping my coffee and trying to appear nonchalant.

She seemed to warm somewhat. A relieved smile curled her lips. "I was worried that you might take your belt to him."

I looked up at her from where I was squatting. "He needs it."

Her smile vanished. "Maybe he needs somebody to understand him instead of whipping him."

I rolled my eyes. "Look," I said, rising to my feet and tossing the dregs of my coffee on the fire. "You and me don't agree on kids. You take care of them. All I want to do is get us to Texas alive. The boy causes me any problems that keeps me from doing my job proper, I'll come down on him like a sunfishing bronco. Otherwise, I won't have nothing to do with him."

Bill glared at me, anger flashing in her eyes. I ignored her as I grabbed my soogan and rolled out my bed.

We pulled out before the sun rose, following the worn trail through the tall Indian Grass. "Somewhere ahead we should hit the Spring River. We'll follow it down to the Neosho," I told Sunny. "I reckon when we hit the Neosho the smart thing is to cross and stay on the west side."

He frowned. "How's that?"

"Easier traveling. The Neosho skirts the Ozark foothills to the east. A couple days from there it hits the Arkansas. Muskogee is just beyond."

Shaking his head, Sunny settled back on the seat wearily. "I sure don't like them river crossings."

I turned my pony south. "Who does?"

Twice during that first day, we spotted dust from north-bound trail drives. As the last cloud of dust disappeared back to the north, Twitch rode up to me and gnawed off a chunk of twist tobacco. He gestured to the cloudless blue sky over us that seemed to stretch forever in all directions. "Kinda lonely out here."

"Yep. Reckon it is."

"Makes a body wish for company."

"Not for me," I replied.

He snorted as I pulled out my bag of Bull Durham. I curled the paper and filled it with tobacco. Using my teeth to tighten the bag, I poked the bag in my vest pocket and rolled my cigarette.

"I don't know about that, Clay. Personally, I figure you kinda taken a shine to that little girl."

I glanced sidelong at him. "Maybe so, but that don't make me wish for company."

"Of course not." He chuckled again and pulled back behind the wagon. " 'Course not."

The next day, we hit the Spring River. From time to time afterward, we spotted small bands of Indians in the distance. That afternoon as half-a-dozen young bucks rode past about half a mile distant, Bill spoke up from her seat beside Sunny, her taut features reflecting her concern. Timmy and Louisa stood behind her, their eyes fixed on the young warriors. "Are they hostile?" She directed the question to Sunny.

Twitch answered her. "Don't reckon there be enough of them to be hostile, Ma'am."

"But there are more of them than us."

Sunny grinned at her, his brilliant white teeth a sharp contrast to his black skin. He laid his hand on the butt of his Winchester. "No, Miss. We gots three of these rifles. Each one holds fifteen cartridges. That means we got forty-five on our side. And them young bucks out there knows it."

Bill sighed. "I see." With a faint smile, she appeared to relax. She whispered to the children. I was too far to hear what she had to say, but whatever it was, they nodded and went back under the wagon bonnet.

While the band made no movement in our direction, every set of eyes in the small party was fixed on us. I had a feeling we might have some visitors after we camped.

I called Twitch up from drag. "I'll ride ahead and find a spot to camp."

Our eyes met, and he read my mind. "Make it a good one."

"Don't worry. If there's a good one, I'll find it."

And I did. For once, Twitch's gloomy prophecies about something always going wrong didn't pan out. I found a spot in a stand of trees in a horseshoe shape formed by the river. The current had cut deep holes and high banks around the curve. The water was too deep to wade, so if anyone decided to come in, they'd either have to swim or come in at the front where there would be a welcome committee of Winchesters waiting.

We camped early. By dark, the fire was out, the horses were tethered, and Bill and the children were bedded down under the wagon. Twitch and I took the front, Sunny the river.

The only sounds were those of the night: Two owls calling, trying to mate, crickets chirruping, leaves rustling with the passing of deer or rooting armadillos, and night birds singing.

After some time, I noticed one particular bird with a song new to me, *see-wee, see-wee, pip, pip, pip.* I didn't think too much of it until I noted that each time he sang, from another part of the prairie came an answering *con-ca-ree, con-ca-ree.*

I hissed at Twitch, who was behind a fallen log twenty feet away. "You hear what I hear?"

"Been listening for the last ten minutes," he whispered. "They're coming closer."

I peered into the night. Beyond the stand of elm and willow in which we lay, the starlight bathed the prairie with a bluish glow in which the shrubs and tall Indian Grass appeared as dark patches.

Our chirping birds and their feathered friends were in the dark patches. I flexed my fingers around the grip of my Winchester, grateful for the fifteen lead plums in the magazine. That plus the five in my Navy Colt gave me a heap of firepower.

Nevertheless, sweat rolled off my forehead and stung my eyes. I dragged my arm across my eyes, and squinted into the night.

The cries came again, closer this time. *See-wee, see-wee, pip, pip, pip.* Moments later, it was answered with *con-ca-ree, con-ca-ree.*

"Get ready," Twitch warned.

I rose to my feet and leaned against the trunk of a large elm, using a low limb as an armrest to steady my rifle.

Off to my left came the cry. *See-wee, see-we—* Without warning, the signal stopped. Moments later came *con-ca-ree, con-ca-ree*, but there was no reply.

I tried to visualize the stealthy moves of the Indians. Had the first one slipped in so close that his cry would give away his position? Or was his silence the signal for attack?

Before I could decide one way or another, the second cry broke the silence once again. *Con-ca-ree, con-c—*. It too was cut off in the middle.

"Twitch."

"Hush. Listen."

I strained to hear the slightest sounds, to catch the faintest of movements.

Moments later, I felt the cold blade of a knife against my throat.

Chapter Nine

The cold starlight bathing the desolate prairie couldn't begin to compare with the icy chill in the pit of my stomach when I felt the razor edge of cold steel against the pulsating vein in the side of my throat. I froze, my arm still resting on the tree limb and my Winchester still tight in my shoulder.

"Not move," a guttural voice whispered in my ear.

I tried to speak, but I couldn't find my voice.

"I friend. No hurt white men."

Finally, I managed to gasp out. "That's good, 'cause I'm your friend."

A long second passed before the knife was removed from my throat. I sighed with relief as the voice said. "Tell old man not to shoot."

"Twitch!"

"Hush. They're still out there."

The voice behind me said, "They go."

I relayed the message to Twitch.

"You don't know that. You didn't even hear them two braves calling out for ten minutes."

"Trust me, Twitch. They're gone."

"Bull."

"Listen to me, Twitch. Someone's here with me. He's a friend. Don't do nothing stupid and start shooting."

Suspicious, Twitch whispered. "What are you talking about?"

"What I said. A man's here with me. He says the Indians are gone."

"What man? Where'd he come from?"

The guttural voice whispered. "Cherokee law. They call me Frank Fivekiller. Call in black man from the river. He got nothing to worry over tonight."

Around the campfire later, we all stared in wonder at Frank Fivekiller, a broad-shouldered black man of about thirty. He wore a slouch hat, no shirt, just a vest, jeans, and moccasins. A knife perched on one hip, a war club on the other, a gunbelt around his waist, and a cartridge belt across his chest. He was an Indian Freedman who had been reared by the Cherokees and was now a member of the Cherokee Lighthorse.

"I heard of you fellers," Twitch drawled. "You old boys keep the law in Indian Territory."

Fivekiller nodded and sipped at the hot coffee Sunny had made. "Them here tonight young Choctaw and Comanche."

"How come they all up and left just like that?" Sunny frowned at Fivekiller.

Without changing his expression, the Freedman laid his large hand on his knife. Sunny nodded. He understood.

Timmy, awed by the large man, whispered. "Were you chasing them?"

"No. I go south to Cane Creek. Word is Joe Buck hides there."

Sunny nodded. "Joe Buck? Ain't he supposed to be a mean one?"

Fivekiller looked at Sunny. "You Freedman?"

Sunny frowned at me.

I explained. "Freedman. A couple years back, the Five Civilized Tribes signed a treaty where the Indians gave their former African slaves citizenship and rights. Those slaves are called Indian Freedman in the nations."

Sunny spoke to Fivekiller. "No. I was born free in Illinois."

Fivekiller frowned. "Ill—i—nois?"

"A state. Up north," Sunny said, pointing to the northeast. "Many, many days."

The Cherokee law officer grunted. "I like to see Ill—i—nois."

Sunny grinned at me. "You know, Clay, I ain't been back home in years. Maybe I ought to see the old folks one more time." He turned back to Fivekiller. "You ever get a break from your law-officering, you just let me know, and the two of us will go back. How does that sound?"

Fivekiller nodded. "That good."

* * *

We invited Frank Fivekiller to ride along with us, but he declined. Next morning, he pulled out astride a deep-chested bay while we were hitching our team. As he said, his business down on Cane Creek with Joe Buck wouldn't wait.

As the sun eased over the horizon, we hit the trail.

Ten minutes later, distant gunfire echoed across the prairie, three distinct rifle reports followed by two gunshots from a handgun.

"What do you reckon?" Twitch called out.

I peered across the gently waving grass to the south. "No telling." I shucked my Winchester and clacked a cartridge in the chamber. "We're not taking any chances."

The rifles boomed again, this time closer.

I backed my pony up to the wagon. "Get inside," I shouted over my shoulder to Bill. "Keep the kids down."

Twitch sat astride his horse on the far side of the wagon. The three of us waited, hammers cocked.

Faint yells rolled across the prairie.

"Sounds like Injuns," Twitch announced.

The shouts grew louder.

"Mad ones, too," Sunny muttered with a wry chuckle.

And then from around a stand of elm trees burst a deep-chested bay, its legs stretching out and pulling the ground under him. Draped over its neck lay Frank Fivekiller.

In the next breath, six warriors swept around the

elms, waving their rifles over their heads and yelping out their war cries.

As one, we cut down on the screaming savages, knocking two from their saddles and almost a third who barely managed to stay in his grass saddle by grabbing his little mustang's flowing mane. The others flared, heading for shelter.

Fivekiller's frightened bay swept past. "Bring him back, Twitch," I shouted, levering another cartridge into the chamber and pulling down on another warrior who was desperately attempting to rein his pony toward the thick stand of elms.

Sunny and I chased the fleeing braves into the nearby forest with the slugs from our Winchesters. Long after they disappeared among the trees, we watched, just in case they decided to swing around and come after us from another direction.

Minutes later, Twitch returned leading the bay with Fivekiller slumped in the saddle, his hands gripping the saddle horn. "Appears he took a couple slugs in the back," Twitch announced.

Fivekiller nodded slowly. "Chickasaw and Choctaw braves. Ambush."

Sunny and I helped him from the saddle. He lay on the blanket Bill had spread while Twitch put water to boil on a hastily built fire.

Sunny eased Fivekiller's vest from the stoic man while Twitch put an edge on his knife. After cleaning the wound, the old man washed his hands and the blade of his knife with our medicinal whiskey, and quickly cut out the slugs.

After binding the Fivekiller's wounds, we tied his bay to the rear of the wagon and loaded the injured man in the wagon despite his protests.

"A couple days will do you wonders, Mr. Five-killer," Bill said.

The next night, we camped beside the tree-lined Neosho River, planning to cross the next morning. Fivekiller, despite the two slugs Twitch carved out of him the previous day, was up and around, much to Bill's displeasure.

"You'll have a relapse," she said to him while we sat at the fire putting ourselves around some of Sunny's tasty venison stew. The children sat on either side of her.

Fivekiller frowned. "Relapse? What be relapse?"

Bill explained.

Fivekiller nodded somberly. "Me no relapse." He pointed to the south. "Me go to Cane Creek."

With a sigh of exasperation, Bill shook her head.

Twitch chuckled. "Different folk out here, Ma'am. Why, I once knew a cowpoke what drove a buggy ninety miles to a sawbones to get a slug dug out of his side. No sooner had the doctor finished sewing him up than he jumped back in the buggy. When the doctor asked where he was going in such an all-fired hurry, he said he was going back to shoot the jasper who had shot him before the no-good owlhoot had a chance to leave town."

Bill glanced at Sunny who nodded. All she could do was shake her head again.

Sunny changed the subject. "I been thinking we best cut logs to float the wagon across the river in the morning. We can't take no chances with the furniture."

I knew exactly what he meant. "Reckon that's as good an idea as I've heard today." I grinned at Louisa, hoping to put her at ease about the river crossing. "You'll float across that river just like you was in one of those big old steamships."

She clapped her hands in delight, but Timmy, refusing to look at me as usual, leaned over and whispered in Bill's ear.

Bill nodded and patted his hand. She whispered to him and gestured to the wagon.

I picked up a small limb. It was too limber for whittling, so I took hold of either end and idly began flexing it, back and forth while the children climbed inside and made ready for bed.

"What was all that with the boy?" I kept my eyes on the limb in front of me.

Her eyes narrowed. "He has a name."

I felt the rebuke in her tone. It rubbed me the wrong way. I straightened the limb. "We all do."

Her words were sharp as a panther's claws. "Would it kill you to use it?"

"It just might."

She stared at me for several seconds, her eyes reflecting frustration. "Timmy's frightened about tomorrow."

I snorted and bent the limb again. "Tell him the fish won't bother him."

Her eyes blazed. "He says he won't cross the river tomorrow."

Keeping my eyes on the slender limb as I bent, then straightened it, I asked, "What do you mean, he won't cross the river?"

She looked at me in disbelief. "What do you think he means? He said he will not cross the river."

I snorted. "He doesn't have a choice."

"He's really scared."

"Now, just how do you know that?" I couldn't keep the sarcasm from my tone.

Her eyes narrowed. "I can tell."

I arched an eyebrow and looked around at her. "He told you?"

"Not in so many words. Maybe if you said more than one or two words to your nephew, you'd find out a few things about him."

I grunted. "I don't need to say more than one or two words to the boy." I hesitated. "All right, to Timmy. Besides, there's nothing for him to be afraid of. The river is only a couple hundred feet wide at this point. We'll tie logs to the axles and float the wagon across. No reason to be afraid. He just needs to grow up," I added, disgusted with the boy's behavior. "What about the girl? She isn't afraid."

Bill glanced over her shoulder at the wagon, then lowered her voice. "She doesn't understand."

"Understand what?" I began to bend and unbend the limb again.

"The way her parents died."

I shook my head. "Now, you lost me."

"What I'm trying to say is that the children's parents died when the ship they were on sank. They drowned. Their bodies were never recovered. So now, every time Timmy sees a river or a lake, he imagines the same thing will happen to him."

I considered her words for several moments. While I was no hand with children, I supposed I could see how a youngster might be worried about the same thing happening to him, but he couldn't let that stop him. "All right. So he's afraid he'll drown like they did. What would you have us do, sit here and never cross any river? Never get back to Texas?" I shook my head. "I'm sorry, Ma'am, but life is full of risks, that is if a jasper plans on going anywhere or doing anything. The boy's going to have to learn. He's got to start growing up."

Her eyes blazed. "Is that all you can say, he's got to grow up? Weren't you a child once?"

I met her eyes. With a slow nod, I replied. "Well, yes, Ma'am, I reckon I was, up until I was about ten."

"But, he's only twelve."

I clenched my teeth and snapped the limb in two. "Out here, Comanches don't care if you're twelve or forty. The boy—sorry, I forgot—Timmy, is no better than anyone else."

"At least you might reassure him like you did Louisa."

"She's smaller, and she's a girl. He's not far from being full-grown. Boys his age out here take on man's responsibilities. It's time for him to learn that instead of whining around."

She glared at me, then spun on her heel and stomped her way up into the wagon.

The four of us sat in silence for several minutes until Sunny decided it was time to hit the sack.

I took the first watch, wanting time to sort the thoughts whirling about in my head.

Was I being unfair to the boy? I didn't think so. Then I wondered if I should tell her about the double eagle. As far as I was concerned, what it boiled down to was he was a sneaky, spoiled brat who had managed to wrap Bill around his little finger.

But that was something she would have to find out for herself.

Chapter Ten

I was awakened well before dawn the next morning by the whinny of a horse. Easing my Colt from its holster, I slowly turned my head in the direction of our ponies.

Silhouetted against the stars was Fivekiller, tightening the cinch on his bay. I rolled out of my blankets. "Mighty early to be leaving," I said.

He grunted, "Long ride to Cane Creek." He touched his fingers to the bandage around his chest. "You be good white people. I not forget you helped Fivekiller."

Our conversation awakened Sunny. "I'll put the fire on and whip up some grub if you want to wait," he said while pulling on his boots.

Fivekiller swung into the saddle. "I go."

By mid-morning, we had moved the wagon down to the shore, felled two logs, and lashed them to the axles of the wagon. We swam the six-horse team to the far shore and put them in harness after which we tied two ropes to the trace chains. The other end of the ropes we strung across the river and tied to the front axles. To keep the wagon from drifting downriver, we lashed a third rope to the bolster of the rear axle and then wrapped it around a thick tree upriver near the shore to be played out as the wagon floated across.

"Looks like we're about set," Sunny said. "I'll stay here and play out the rope."

Across the river, Twitch waved. I waved back, then turned to Bill who was back at the campfire with Louisa. I didn't see Timmy, but I figured he was wandering along the shore somewhere. "Get the kids and climb in," I shouted.

She nodded.

I planned to swim my pony alongside the wagon, just in case something unexpected took place. I looked around to see Bill and Louisa running toward us. Now what?

Bill was breathless. "Clay! Timmy's gone. I can't find him."

"What?" I stared at her in disbelief.

Sunny muttered. "Twitch said something bad would happen."

I shot him a dirty look. Now, Twitch had Sunny believing all those gloomy warnings.

Bill nodded jerkily and pointed upriver. "After breakfast, he wanted to explore along the river bank. I told him not to go too far. I found his tracks, but they disappeared in the Indian Grass. He didn't answer when I called. He could be hurt."

I muttered a curse under my breath.

Swinging into the saddle, I rode along the shoreline. Sure enough, there were his tracks, and just as Bill had said, they led along the shore until they cut into the Indian Grass around the first bend. A few stems of the tall grass were bent or broken, marking his trail.

Reining up, I cupped my hand to my mouth and shouted. The only answer was the soft wind rustling the leaves overhead. "That blasted little . . ." If I could have put my hands on him at that moment, he wouldn't have been able to sit for a month.

For several moments, I studied the prairie over which we had journeyed. A few miles distant stretched a line of trees. The boy could be anywhere out there, a half-mile or thirty feet. I glanced over my shoulder. The only choice I saw was to take the wagon across the river. They could continue down river while I came back and ran the boy down. Tracking him through the grass would be painstakingly slow.

When I returned to the wagon, Bill was holding Louisa's hand. Both watched as I rode up. I could see the accusation in Bill's eyes. "He ran away," she announced flatly. "He told Louisa he was going back to Philadelphia."

I looked at the little girl. "Why didn't you tell us, Louisa?"

In a small, timid voice, she said, "Timmy told me not to. He said you wouldn't be my uncle if I told."

The impact of her answer hit me in the chest. At

the same time, I recognized the fact that Timmy was a smarter, and sneakier youngster than I thought. He had manipulated his little sister slicker than calf slobber. I glanced at Bill, then back to the girl. "Nothing will ever keep me from being your uncle, Louisa. Remember that, okay?"

She nodded.

"Good. Now, you climb up in the wagon. We'll take it across the river, and then I'll come back and find Timmy." I deliberately ignored Bill. I had grown tired of the accusing looks she gave me.

I crossed my fingers, hoping that Twitch's gloomy warnings would not bear fruit on this crossing.

The crossing went just the way we planned. We pulled the wagon ashore and backed the horses up to it. After hitching them to the wagon, I swung into the saddle. "I'll be back as soon as I can. Just stay with the river to Muskogee. From there bear south to Tuskahoma on the Kiamichi River. It's a few days. If I haven't caught up by then, follow the Kiamichi on down to the Red River."

Twitch spoke up. "I know the way from there."

With a chuckle, I replied. "You should."

Sunny nodded. "You take care."

I winked at him. "I plan to."

As soon as the wagon rolled out, I swam the river to find Timmy.

Last time I had seen him was just after breakfast. That was five hours earlier. He could be anywhere by now.

Reining up by the edge of the Indian Grass, I scanned the vast prairie stretching in every direction. My stomach knotted. He could get lost out there and no one would ever find him. I studied the line of trees stretching across the horizon a few miles distant. I couldn't help worrying about the youngster, and at the same time wanting to tan his hide.

I studied the grass. If I moved cautiously, I might find enough broken or bent stems that would at least give me a general idea of his direction.

Eyes fixed on the grass, I rode parallel to what I believed was his trail. It zig-zagged across the prairie in the general direction of the tree line. Then I lost it altogether. Despite circling, I failed to cut his sign, so I turned my attention to the stand of elm and oak trees.

"Maybe that's where he headed," I muttered, urging my pony into a running walk.

When I reached the trees, I cut west, keeping my eyes on the ground made soft by years of rotting leaves. My hopes soared when I found his tracks. They led into the trees. I followed, intent on the trail, figuring I would run across him at any moment. Unexpectedly, the tracks took a sharp turn and then the boy began running.

I reined up. My heart thudded against my chest as I stared in alarm at the horse tracks obliterating Timmy's. I muttered a curse. Unshod ponies. That meant Indian horses.

I studied the sign. Half-a-dozen or so ponies. They must have been hiding in the trees, watching Timmy as he approached. There was no sign he had been harmed. Easing forward, I studied the tracks. Best I could tell, two of the party came up on either side of the running boy and grabbed his arms, lifting him from the ground.

I followed the sign to the edge of the trees. Their trail through the grass was as clear as if a herd of buffalo had trampled it.

They were heading west, into the Cherokee Nation. From their sign, they were not in a hurry. I tried to push Timmy from my mind, to concentrate on the trail, but the feelings churning inside of me were too strong. Was I following a war party? Or was it simply a hunting party?

I guessed the latter, for had it been a war party, they would have bashed out Timmy's brains and left him where they found him. No, a hunting party seemed the logical answer, a hunting party was returning home and seized the opportunity to provide a son to some Comanche or Choctaw family who had lost a young warrior fighting the white man.

The longer I stayed with the trail, the more certain I became that the small band had a definite destination in mind. The trail didn't waver in its west-by-northwest direction.

Not long before sunset, I dismounted and gave my horse a breather. I loosened the cinch, poured water in my hat and let him drink. "We'll rest here until dark, then move out." Tonight was a full moon, and I didn't reckon I'd have any trouble following the sign of six or seven ponies.

* * *

An hour after moonrise, I rode out. The full moon lit the prairie like day. The trail was obvious, and I followed it at a trot. Around midnight, I spotted a darker shadow on the horizon.

Trees.

I tightened the reins, slowing my pony to a walk. I sniffed the air, trying to pick up the odor of wood-smoke. There was no breeze, which was good and bad. Good because, if the small party was camped in the trees, their ponies couldn't pick up the smell of mine, and bad because I couldn't pick up the odor of their campfire.

Off to my left, a coyote howled. An answering cry sounded from behind. The sounds of the night filled my ears, crickets, and the squeal of rabbits. I kept moving at a casual pace, not wanting to startle any of the creatures into silence.

When I figured I was a few hundred yards from the stand of trees, I halted. Ground reining my horse, I moved forward on foot. So far, I had not spotted a fire. Every few feet, I dropped to one knee and listened, expecting the nicker of a horse.

I heard nothing.

After what seemed like hours, I reached the stand of elm and oak. I dashed from the tall grass to one of the trees and pressed up against the trunk. Bright shafts of moonlight lanced through the treetops, splashing their pale glow on the forest floor like a handful of spilled marbles. I peered into the darkness.

Best I could figure, the stand was half-a-mile or so in length, and about the same in width. I could see no sign of a fire, nor hear a sound that suggested the party had camped here.

I scratched my head. They had to be somewhere nearby. They had no reason to continue riding deep into the night. Then I had an idea. Holstering my handgun, I shinnied about thirty or forty feet up a tall elm.

That's when I spotted them.

A mile or so west, a faint glow came from a basin in the prairie. Probably a waterhole, I guessed. That's why they passed up the shelter of the trees. My hopes surged. Hastily I returned to my pony and took up the trail.

I figured that once I was close enough, I could slip up on the camp and while they were sleeping, try to figure out how I would go about getting Timmy.

The basin in which they camped was forty or fifty yards across. In the middle was a good-sized water hole. Next to it, a large fire blazed. Meat impaled on spits sizzled as it broiled.

To my surprise, most of the warriors were awake. I counted five braves and two youths from where I lay on my belly in the tall grass. Timmy sat slumped near one warrior who appeared older than the others. As I watched, one brave shouted at Timmy and gestured to the fire. Timmy climbed to his feet and picked up a spit of roasting meat. He started back to the warrior, but as he passed two young Indians about his own age, one of them stuck his foot out and tripped Timmy.

He fell and dropped the meat, which enraged the

warrior. He jumped to his feet and shouted at Timmy, at the same time kicking the boy's legs.

I resisted the urge to start shooting. I could probably get a couple, but Timmy would be in the middle of the fight, and I couldn't take a chance on his catching a slug. No, all I could do was wait for the right opportunity.

The angry warrior grabbed another spit of broiling meat and returned to his blankets, shoving Timmy down beside him. In the meantime, the two Indian boys began teasing and taunting Timmy, nudging him with their toes, shouting at him. One reached down and yanked Timmy's hair.

With a cry of anger, Timmy jumped to his feet and, arms flailing, charged one of the boys. With cat-like reflexes, the Indian youth easily sidestepped and tripped Timmy as he rushed past, sending the boy sprawling in the dirt.

The whole band laughed, but Timmy jumped back to his feet and tried again. And again, the lithe and quick Indian boy made the angry youth miss.

Then it got to be a game for the Indian boys, jumping around, taunting Timmy to rush them, then sending him spilling to the ground.

I kept hoping the young boy would connect with one of those wildly flailing arms, but he never did.

Finally, too exhausted to move, Timmy lay where he last fell, unable to respond to their continued taunts.

I muttered through clenched teeth. "Just hang on, Boy. Hang on. I'll get you out of there somehow."

Chapter Eleven

It was one thing to say I was going to get him away from his captors, and quite another to do it. There was no question in my mind that I could kill all five of the braves before they could respond, but other than taunting Timmy, they had not hurt him. Killing wasn't natural with me, although I'm certain that along the line somewhere, someone might have died from one of my slugs. But it wasn't as if I went looking to plant some jasper in the ground.

Even as I lay in the grass and watched the camp, the warriors, having tired of having fun with Timmy, sprawled on their blankets. Then I noticed that each of them tied his war pony to his ankle with a length of leather reata, a practice that prevented the animal from grazing too far during the night.

That gave me an idea. Outrageous, but it could work. If it didn't, I still had my Navy Colt and my

Winchester. If it came right down to killing to rescue Timmy, I would.

My plan was simple, like me. Once they were all sound asleep, I'd ride in hooting and hollering, firing my gun, doing my best to scare the bejeebees out of those Indian ponies and send them racing across the prairie dragging their owners with them. That should distract them long enough for me to steal Timmy away.

I was doing my best to convince myself the plan could work.

Maybe.

After I picked up Timmy, and before we headed out in the opposite direction, I'd drop a handful of slugs in the fire. That should divert their attention a few more minutes.

Maybe.

I knew the idea was risky, but I reckon it was even more of a risk to wait until the next day. For all I knew, their village was only a few miles distant.

Swinging into the saddle, I tore off a corner of my neckerchief and tied it around a handful of cartridges. I stuffed the small bag in my vest pocket. I whispered to my pony. "Okay, Boy, let's go. Nice and easy. You'll know when to run." I drew a deep breath. My heart thudded against my chest.

I could feel my pulse begin to race as I drew near the fire. I flexed my fingers about the butt of my Colt. Just as I reached the top of the basin, an Indian pony nickered.

His owner, groggy from sleep, rose to one elbow.

That's when I cut loose. "Yeeeehah!" With a wild rebel yell, I drove my horse down into the basin, firing my Colt.

Startled, the Indian ponies bolted in every direction, dragging the hapless warriors after them. Two were dragged through the water hole, two others' ropes crossed, slamming them into each other, and a fifth was dragged kicking and screaming through the fire.

"Timmy!"

The boy had leapt to his feet. When he spotted me, he waved frantically. I swept around the fire and veered in his direction, holstering my handgun and holding out my arm.

He grabbed it and together, we swung him up on the rump of my horse. I wheeled around, threw the cartridges in the fire, and dug my heels into my horse. "Grab hold of me, Boy," I shouted over my shoulder. "And don't let go."

From out of nowhere, one of the Indian boys leaped at us. Timmy kicked him in the face, sending the boy sprawling to the ground. We raced from the camp. Suddenly, a warrior rose from the ground directly in front of me.

I ran over him.

Within minutes, they would be on our trail, so I headed north, planning on making a wide swing back to the south after losing them.

Behind us, the cartridges exploded, adding to the

confusion of the night. With luck, by the time they gathered their thoughts, we'd have a good lead.

With Timmy hanging on to me tighter than green bark on a tree, I pushed my pony hard for three or four miles before slowing to a walking two step. We couldn't afford to run him into the ground.

Timmy whispered in alarm. "What's wrong? Why'd you slow down?"

"Got to save him in case they spot us." I glanced over my shoulder. The moonlight bathed the prairie with a pale glow. I squinted at the darker shadows against the background of grass. What few I spotted didn't seem to be moving.

An hour later, we ran across a shallow creek lined with trees, flowing east. I guessed it emptied into the Neosho River.

Reining up in the trees, I said. "Hop down. We got to give the pony a rest."

Timmy refused to loosen his grip on me.

"It's all right, Boy. Slide off and stretch your legs. Fill up your belly with water. I got nothing to eat."

Reluctantly, he released his grip and slid to the ground. I dismounted and loosened the cinch and led the pony to the creek. I rationed his water. After a few moments, I pulled him away and tied the reins to a tree. Then I dropped to my belly and drank long and deep from the cool water of the small creek.

The moon was dropping in the west, and the shadows cast by the trees fell over us. Despite the shadows, I could see that Timmy had been used pretty good. His shirt was grimy and soiled. The collar had been ripped off, and holes were worn in the knees of his trousers. He looked like he'd been ridden hard and put away wet. "How do you feel, Boy?"

He looked up at me. His lips quivered, and when a piece of the moonlight slashed across his face, I saw the tears in his eyes. He bit his lip to keep from crying, but now that the frightening ordeal was behind him, he was unable to control his emotions. He burst out crying.

My first thought was to tell him to stop crying like a baby and act like a man, but Bill's words from the night before rang in my ears. He was an Eastern boy, dumped in the West fresh from civilization. I chastised myself. Maybe I should have thought of that sooner.

The little twelve-year-old stood facing me, his fists clenched at his side, doing his best to control the tears rolling down his cheeks. I laid my hand on his shoulder. "That's all right, Timmy. Cry it out."

Suddenly he lunged forward, burying his face in my chest and wrapping his arms around me. I'd never been in that sort of situation before. I didn't know what to do, so I just patted him on the head to calm him down just like I would a frightened calf.

Finally, his sobs lessened.

I pulled off my neckerchief with the missing corner and handed it to him. "Here. Dry your eyes."

He nodded against my chest as he took the neckerchief and dried his eyes. He stepped back and blew his nose several times, then offered me the neckerchief. "Here."

I eyed the neckerchief skeptically. "That's all right, Boy. You keep it. Now, you feel like riding?"

We rode until mid-morning, forting up in a motte of oaks in the middle of the grassy prairie. We could see miles in every direction, which meant we would also be easy to spot upon leaving the trees. My stomach was gnawing against my backbone. Timmy was leaning against an ancient oak. "Hungry?"

I noticed that arrogant little curl that he used to wear on his lips was gone. "Sure am. Can't you shoot something?"

I tossed him the canteen. "Drink. Can't take a chance on shooting. The sound carries for miles."

He cast a worried look over our back trail. "You think they're still following?"

"Yep. I shamed them last night. They won't rest until they reclaim their honor."

He frowned at me. "I don't understand."

"I stole you from them."

"But they kidnapped me."

"Makes no difference to them. Once you're their property, it's forever." I tightened the cinch. "Let's move out. We'll find some grub when we reach the river."

We rode easy, saving my pony. I didn't know how much he had left so I wanted to conserve him for an emergency.

And one came in late afternoon just as we spotted the tree line of the Neosho River.

Timmy cried out. "Clay! Behind us. Indians."

I looked around to see five or six warriors on the crest of a hill some two miles behind. They spotted us at the same time.

"Hold on, Boy." I dug my heels into the horse's flank and we raced toward the river. Within a few hundred yards, the horse stumbled, caught himself, and continued the mad dash for the river. But I knew he was just about all tuckered out. I gauged us to be less than a mile from the river.

The tall Indian Grass swept past as the gallant little pony stretched out his legs and pulled the ground under him. We topped a hill and spotted the river below. I threw a hasty glance over my shoulder before we dropped off the hill.

The yelping warriors were only a mile behind now.

The pony began to labor, his breath coming in raw gasps.

I took in the river at a glance. Beyond, the timber grew thick, and the prairie gave away to the foothills of the Ozarks.

We could not outrun the pursuing savages, nor could we fight them off. They were too many, and they were on the hunt.

In the bend of the river, I spotted a thick tangle of logs bunched up like a stack of hay. If we could work a log loose, then we could float downriver. But first, we had to give our pursuers the dodge.

Timmy screamed when we hit the river. As soon as

the horse started to swim, I pushed Timmy off and followed, taking time to grab my rope, the canteen, and the Winchester. "Swim for the logs," I shouted. Then it dawned on me that he might not be able to swim.

"Timmy," I shouted, treading water and looking for him. To my relief, I spotted the boy already halfway to the logjam. Moments later, I pulled up beside him. His eyes were wide with fear. "Easy, easy. You're all right."

He nodded jerkily.

"We're going to hide in the logs," I explained. "If we're lucky, they'll follow my horse. That'll give us time to get on downriver."

We worked our way behind a large log. I quickly looped the rope and canteen over my shoulder. Without warning, the Indians hit the river. Howling like banshees, they charged over, and, disappearing into the forest, took up pursuit of my horse. I prayed that the pony kept on running.

Unfortunately, within scant moments, two warriors emerged from the forest and pulled up on the shore, studying the river. I muttered a curse. They had already found my pony. So much for my prayers. "Quick, farther back in the logs," I whispered urgently.

Timmy looked around at me, dread evident on his face. "How?"

"Take a breath, go under one log, then come up. Then do it again." Fear filled his eyes, but he nodded and went under.

Within minutes, we were hidden in a small hollow deep in the tangle of logs, and just in time, for two young warriors suddenly appeared on the shore, studying the jumble of logs.

Chapter Twelve

"**Q**uiet," I whispered.

Through a crack between two logs, I could see the warriors from the shoulders up. They were studying the logjam intently.

Timmy's eyes were wide with fear. I couldn't help remembering what Bill had told me about the boy's parents. I nodded and whispered. "Don't worry. I'm right here with you."

He gulped and nodded, his face reflecting his anxiety. Suddenly, his eyes grew wide and his hand slipped off the log. He grabbed desperately at it to keep from going underwater, and when he did, he made a loud splash.

The warriors heard the noise. One gestured in our direction.

I glared at Timmy who was pointing behind me. He mouthed the word, "snake." I looked around to see a yellow and black water snake as big around as my wrist curled on a log less than two feet from my face.

Holding to the log with one hand, I brought the muzzle of the Winchester from the water and jabbed it at the snake. It hissed and struck at the muzzle. At the same time, I felt the logs shift. I glanced around in time to see one of the warriors picking his way across the logs toward us.

I jabbed at the snake again. This time, the snake plopped in the water and swam quickly toward the shore, curling over the logs and finally squirming through a crack between two of them. Moments later, the warrior on the logjam gave a startled shout which was followed by a gunshot.

Peering up through the logs, I saw one brave holding the dead snake up for the other warrior to see. I nodded to Timmy. "They're leaving," I whispered. "Be quiet."

As we watched, the other warriors appeared on the shore. Half went upriver, the others down, searching the shore for sign of us.

Timmy uttered not a single word the rest of the day.

Night settled over the river. I figured we had an hour before the waning moon rose. We had to move fast. We eased from under the logjam. Timmy headed for shore, but I stopped him. "Stay in the water. Don't give them any tracks. Here, hold this." I handed him the Winchester and canteen and uncoiled my rope. After some tussling, I managed to free two logs and lash them together at each end with a length of rope. The

stubs of broken limbs held the two trunks apart enough
for us to fit in between. I piled broken limbs over the
logs to hide our faces.

I put Timmy in front of me. I knew he was scared,
and I couldn't begin to imagine the kind of horror in
his mind. "Hook your arm around that limb." He nodded and did as I instructed. "I'm right here behind
you." I laid the Winchester and canteen as well as the
remainder of the rope between two limbs to keep them
out of the water. Then we pushed away from the logjam just as the moon rose and cast its pale glow over
the river.

The gentle current carried us downriver. From time
to time, we ran aground at a bend in the river and
were forced to shove our poor excuse for a raft back
into the current.

Two hours later, we spotted a fire ahead on the east
bank.

"There they are," I whispered. "Keep your head
down."

I could see no figures moving around the campfire.
I crossed my fingers that they were all sleeping. As
we drew near, a figure suddenly appeared in front of
the fire and headed through the trees for the river.

As we drew even with the fire, the warrior emerged
from the trees and halted on the riverbank. I couldn't
see his eyes, but I had the feeling he was staring directly at us. Moments later, he waded into the water
and started swimming lazily for our logs. I reached for
the Winchester. I grabbed the muzzle, planning on using the butt as a club if necessary.

Peering over the top of the log, I watched as the warrior drew closer. He appeared to be in no hurry. I couldn't help realizing the irony of the situation. We were about to be discovered just because an Indian brave decided on a moonlight swim.

He drew closer. I lowered my head.

Moments later, one hand slapped against the log, then another. A head rose from the water, and then he spotted Timmy. Before he could utter a sound, I drove the butt into his temple with both hands. With a soft groan, he slipped under the surface of the river.

We drifted all night. Timmy was scared, tired, hungry, on the verge of exhaustion. With the sunrise, I looked for a spot we could go ashore without leaving a trail. Finally, I spied what I had been looking for. Another log had been washed ashore during some past flood. One end lay in the water, the other extended beyond the shoreline to a low bank covered with grass.

"There," I said. "See that log?"

The young boy nodded.

"Swim to it. Climb it to the bank. Don't step on the shore." I started to follow, but I realized if the Indians found our two logs lashed together, they would have an idea where we were. Quickly, I slashed the ropes, then swam for shore with my gear.

Despite my wet boots and the slick log, I made it up to the grassy bank without falling. From there we headed downriver, taking care to stay in the grass. Ahead I spotted a stand of oak and elm. We had to stop and rustle us up something to eat.

For the first time since that first night, luck decided to take a seat on our shoulders. At the edge of the trees grew a thick tangle of blooming elderberries. Timmy grabbed them by the handful and jammed them in his mouth.

"Don't gorge yourself, Boy. You'll make yourself sick." He hesitated and looked up at me.

"Eat slow. Your belly's shrunk. It can't handle too much too fast."

"Yes, Sir," he whispered.

That was the first time he had ever called me, sir. The boy seemed to have grown up considerably, not that he'd had any choice. I just hoped he could handle the next few days. They were going to be mighty hard.

I dropped the Winchester and rope inside the trees and headed for the river. I had spotted some *wapato* blooming up river. Maybe I could find some nearby.

At this stretch of the river, the grass ran right up to the water's edge. I glanced upriver, then down. That's when I spotted the *wapato*, green plants with arrowhead-shaped leaves on slender stalks three or four feet high. On the roots below the water, potato-like tubers formed, floating to the surface when broken from the root.

I quickly gathered a hatful of the small round potatoes and returned to where I had left Timmy picking berries. We moved into the middle of the small stand of elm for our first food in two days. Berries and tubers aren't much of a meal by any standards, but for us, it was like dining at the Palmer House in Chicago.

Timmy looked up at me. "Can we rest here awhile?"

His eyes were hollow, his face drawn, and his voice plaintive.

I gave him a reassuring grin. "Yeah. You sleep. I'll watch."

With a wan smile, he lay on his side, and in the next second, he was asleep.

Leaning against a tree, I watched our back trail. I don't know how many times I dozed, but the last time I awakened, it was dark. Timmy was still sleeping.

I rose and studied the moonlit prairie around us. I could see nothing unusual or alarming. Shaking my head, I returned to the tree against which I had been leaning. Might as well get some sleep too.

In the bright light of day the next morning, I could see exactly how much the last few days had taken from both Timmy and me. Our clothes were tattered and dirty. It was probably the dirt holding the rags together.

Timmy had some color back in his face. I couldn't tell about mine from the reflection in the river because my whiskers were growing long.

In preparation for our move downriver, we gathered more berries and *wapatoes*. I couldn't help noticing Timmy as he waded through the water harvesting the small tubers and filling his pockets. He wasn't the same boy who had come in on the train from Philadelphia.

As far south as the eye could follow the river, trees grew thick on either side. As long as we remained in the trees, we could see the Indians before they spotted us. I glanced at my boots. Western boots were made for riding, not walking. The most I could make in them was four, maybe five miles before my arches completely broke down.

And I had no material for moccasins.

Still, we couldn't stay here. So we struck out.

Mid-morning, my arches started throbbing. I knew I couldn't keep going much longer before shucking my boots. If I did that, I wouldn't have to worry about my arches, only about cutting my feet to shreds. My only other choice was knocking the heels off the boots.

"How are you doing?" I looked down at Timmy.

His face was drenched with perspiration. "Fine."

"Tired?"

He nodded.

"We'll take break in a few minutes. How does that sound?"

He grinned. "Good. If you think we should," he added.

Then the Good Lord smiled on us.

Back to the west, a solitary rider appeared on the horizon. I frowned. From the way he sat his pony, he was Indian, but he wore white man's clothes. Probably a half-breed. "Wonder what he's doing out here all by himself," I mumbled.

For whatever reason, he seemed to be heading in our direction. That's when I had an idea.

I stopped under a large oak and quickly outlined my plan to Timmy. He was going to be my bait. "Let him see you. When he gets close enough, take off running. Make sure he comes under this oak. I'll be up there with my rope, and when he comes under, I'll snag him."

For a few moments, Timmy hesitated. I cleared my throat. "I'm not crazy about the idea either, Timmy. But, it's better than going back with the Indians, isn't it?"

He swallowed hard and nodded. "I'll do it." I was proud of him at that moment. He was scared. That was obvious. But he saw he had a job to do, and he pushed his fear aside.

After I positioned him at the edge of the trees, I climbed into the spreading oak with my rope and waited.

Ten minutes later, Timmy shouted and raced under me. Behind him came a galloping horse with a rider leaning over the animal's neck. Just before the pony reached the oak, the rider jerked him to a halt. He pushed his round brimmed hat to the back of his head and looked up at me. "Why, Clay Morgan, what the Sam Hill are you doing up in that tree?"

I blinked once, twice, then I recognized the grinning face of Joe Bunting, half-white, half-Tonkawa. "Joe Bunting! Where in the blazes did you come from?"

"Well, stop acting like an old he-coon and come on down. I'll tell you, but don't take long, there's a passel of Choctaw and Comanche back north searching the country mighty hard."

After sliding to the ground, I introduced Timmy and quickly filled Joe in on our situation. He looked us up and down, then shook his head. "I reckon you be the one they's looking for. Well, we best move, and move fast, but neither of you looks like he could walk another ten feet. You ride. I'll hold to the saddle."

He got no argument from me, or Timmy.

We headed south, moving at a rapid pace. Once or twice during the afternoon, we paused at some of the small tributaries of the Neosho, but only for a few minutes.

We made an early camp in a thick stand of willows on the bank of a small creek. Joe shaved jerky in a small pot and boiled us some broth while we gnawed on strips of the dried buffalo. After we finished the broth, he brewed some coffee, and by sundown, while we weren't stuffed like a Thanksgiving turkey, our stomachs had stopped gnawing at our backbones.

We pulled out at midnight. We traveled hard the next two days. Sunrise on the third day, we caught our first glimpse of Muskogee.

By noon, I had outfitted us with new duds and new ponies as well as bacon, flour, coffee, sugar, and jerky for our trip. From the livery, I learned that Twitch and the wagon had passed through a few days earlier.

Joe Bunting and Timmy had remained astride their horses while I spoke with the liveryman. "What did you find out, Clay?" Joe asked when I returned.

I nodded south. "They're three days ahead of us." I nodded to Timmy, "Let's head to Tuskahoma." Looking up at Joe, I grinned. "I'm much obliged, Joe. You pulled our bacon from the fire."

Joe shrugged. "Just happened to be passing by." He paused and glanced to the south. "You got no objection, I'll ride along with you."

I swung into the saddle. "I was hoping you would."
I glanced at Timmy who sat on the small horse I had
picked for him. "Ready?"

He nodded. "I guess. I never rode a horse by myself
before."

Joe grinned. "You just keep the back straight and
your boots in the stirrups. You'll do good."

Tuskahoma was four or five days by wagon. I figured we could make it in two, at the most three days
even with a green rider.

Chapter Thirteen

Though we needed to ride hard, we couldn't because of Timmy. Every time we pushed our ponies to a trot, he bounced up and down in the saddle like a rubber ball. It hurt me to watch him. By the time we took a noon break, he could barely walk, and then it was bowlegged.

Joe winked at me, and I grinned back. We both sympathized with the young boy, but there was no way we could make it easier on him. To his credit, he did not complain except to admit that he was sore all over. "My rear, my insides, and my legs burn." He paused and forced a grin. "I sure will be glad when we camp tonight," he added.

He was so exhausted that night that he fell asleep before he finished his supper of bacon and gravy. Next morning, the young boy could barely roll out of his bedroll because his muscles were so sore.

"Walk around, Boy," Joe advised him. "Work out the soreness."

Timmy might have been sore, but he had a mighty hefty appetite that morning. Of course, he ate standing up.

We made better time the second day, and by the third, he was getting the hang of riding, managing to match the rhythm of his horse most of the time.

I couldn't help feeling a sense of pride in the youth. He was a far cry from the arrogant and selfish youngster who climbed off the train in Kansas City. In fact, I told myself, I didn't even mind that he was my nephew.

Two or three times, we spotted small bands of Indians in the distance. On the third day, one band spotted us. Joe rode out to palaver.

"Choctaws," he said upon returning. "Heading north to their village." He glanced at Timmy. "They be mighty restless."

"Trouble?"

He nodded. "Looks that way." He hesitated, then added. "Especially back down south."

A chill ran up my spine. *The wagon!*

Joe saw the look of consternation on my face. He nodded. "That's what I was thinking."

I looked at Timmy. "Think you can ride that pony hard?"

He gulped and glanced shyly at Joe before nodding to me. "I—I think so."

"If you feel like you're going to get in trouble, let me know. We'll slow down."

We put our ponies into a lope, eating up the miles. Timmy held his reins in one hand and with the other, clung to the saddle horn. Sometimes he bounced, sometimes he fell into the flow of the gait. The contortions on his face reflected the agony he was going through.

Just before sundown, we pulled up on the crest of one of the foothills of the Ozarks. In the distance, we spotted a campfire and the wagon.

I grinned at Timmy. "Well, Timmy, we made it. There they are."

Naturally, they were all happy to see us. Bill and Louisa treated Timmy like a returning hero, and to my mind, he was pretty close to one for all the discomfort he had endured without complaint the last several days.

Sunny whipped up a supper of fried venison, succotash, red-eye gravy, and hot biscuits. While we put ourselves around the grub, Timmy regaled them with our adventure.

After Bill put Timmy and Louisa to bed, she returned to the campfire and poured herself another cup of coffee. "I can't get over how he's changed. He's like a different boy."

Joe grinned at me, but remained silent. I tried to explain it to her. "It's the West. It's a fire that will either temper a jasper to a razor-edge sharpness or burn him up. It's a hard teacher, and sometimes if you don't learn the lesson, you don't get another chance. Timmy made it. He's got a ways to go, but he's headed in the right direction."

She studied me several moments, a thoughtful expression on her face. "Maybe I was wrong."

I frowned. "About what?"

She smiled sheepishly, "About you, about the way you treated him."

Twitch drawled. "The proof's in the pudding, Ma'am."

Sunny nodded.

When we pulled out early next morning, Joe Bunting left us. He had business in Caffreys on Boggy Creek over in Choctaw Country. For the next few days, we stayed with the Kiamichi River down to its confluence with the Red River and its smooth bluffs of red sandstone. Decades of wagons had cut a deep and narrow passage through the cliffs on either side.

Standing on the north bank of the river, Sunny, Twitch, and I studied the sandy riverbed, which was a half-mile wide at this point. A narrow stream of water wound its tortuous path down through the center of the riverbed. Our primary concern was quicksand, a danger for which the Red was notorious.

"Well, Boys," I said, nodding to the cut in the bluffs of red sandstone on the far side of the river. "Yonder's our path into Texas."

"Sure wish we was over there now instead of here," Twitch muttered.

"Well, we ain't," Sunny replied. "So we best gets us an armful of branches and mark a trail across."

"Sounds smart to me," Twitch answered.

A tiny voice sounded from behind us. "Can I go with you?"

I looked around to see Timmy standing there. My first impulse was to refuse his request, but then I reminded myself just how far he had come. "Stay with us. Don't wander off, you hear?"

A broad grin split his face. He nodded gleefully. "Yes, Sir."

Twitch and Sunny grinned at me.

On foot, we spent the next hour picking our way across the river, skirting beds of quicksand and poking branches and small limbs in the sand.

Upon returning to the north bank, Twitch surveyed the trail we had laid out. "Crooked as a snake," he said.

"Maybe so," Sunny replied, climbing up on the wagon seat. "I would sooner have it crooked and hard instead of soupy and straight."

Twitch and me looped our ropes around the front axle, adding our two ponies to the six pulling the wagon.

"Remember, Boys. Once we start, we best move fast. That wagon and its goods is mighty heavy." I looked at Bill who had taken her seat beside Sunny. Her face was pale. Louisa stood behind her. "Hold on, Ladies. Once we start, we're not slowing down." I turned to Timmy who was astride his pony. "You stay right at my side. If your horse hits quicksand, get off fast. When you hit the ground, roll. Spread out like that, you won't sink as fast. I'll get a rope to you."

He swallowed hard and nodded nervously.

I looked our little party over. "Ready?"

Sunny nodded.

"Let's go," I shouted, driving my heels into my pony's flank.

We hit the sandy bed on the run, horses straining in the harness, ears back, eyes wide, sensing the danger. The wagon wheels cut deeply into the sand. "Keep them horses going, Sunny," I shouted. "Don't let them slack up."

He didn't reply. He was too busy handling the reins, his fingers trying to sense the horses' next move through the leather ribbons.

The watercourse in the middle of the bed was forty or fifty feet wide, but less than a foot deep. We hit it at a gallop. Geysers of water sprayed out on either side of the lumbering wagon.

Her face white as the clouds overhead, Bill was clinging to the wagon seat with both hands. Louisa had dropped to her knees and clutched the back of the seat desperately. As the wagon emerged from the water, a rear wheel hit a small hole of quicksand we had overlooked and dropped almost a foot, but Sunny laid

the leather to the frightened horses, and with a surge
of power, they pulled the wagon free.

Ahead, the red bluffs along the south shore loomed
nearer. I kept my eyes focused on the narrow passage
that cut its way through the red sandstone. With each
second, it grew closer until finally we pulled out of
the sand and clattered onto the hard sandstone that
marked the south shore of the river. We reined up.
The red bluffs towered above us.

As one, we all sighed with relief. I turned to Bill.
"Well, how did you like you first taste of quicksand?"

The color was returning to her cheeks. She glanced
back at the broad expanse of sand and shook her head.
"It was—something."

Twitch pointed to the trail ahead of us. It made a
gentle curve to the left. "If I remember right," he
drawled, "this here cut swings to the left, then back to
the right where it opens out to a stand of oaks. That
would be a right prime spot to noon."

We removed our ropes from the front axle. "Sounds
good to me," I said as I coiled my rope and tied it to
the saddle. I removed my hat and dragged the back of
my arm across my forehead to wipe away the sweat.
"Everyone set? Then let's go get us some grub."

I led out, feeling right pert that we had managed
the Red River without any problems. Behind me, the
wagon wheels hammered on the sandstone. The ech-
oes bounced off the twenty-foot walls on either side
of us.

Twitch was right. We swung left, then thirty feet
ahead the trail took a right turn. I glanced down at

Timmy who was riding beside me. The sun over the last few days had darkened his skin. "How are you doing?"

He looked up and grinned. "That was scary back there."

I chuckled. "But we made it."

A trace of excitement edged his voice. "Are there any other rivers like that before we get to my grand-father's?"

"Not like that one. There are rivers—big ones—but they'll be heading the same direction as us." I reined my pony to the right as we entered the turn.

Moments later, we came out of the cut, and I froze, unable to believe my eyes.

Directly in front of me sitting on their horses were five bearded gents, pointing their guns at us.

I could only gape in stunned disbelief at the one in front of the five. Sitting there grinning like a he-coon with an ear of corn was Joe Sterling, back from the dead.

Chapter Fourteen

The blistering heat of the noonday sun seemed to reverberate with a deathly silence.

I was dumbfounded. My brain raced, searching frantically for a logical explanation for what my eyes were seeing.

Joe tipped his black hat to the back of his head with the tip of his finger. The grin on his face faded. "Hello, Clay. I could say I was surprised to see you, but I'm not. I've been waiting. You made good time."

Twitch pulled up beside me as I stammered. "J—Joe? But, you're—I mean, I saw you fall in the river. You were shot. You—"

He laughed, a cruel mocking laugh. "Maybe I missed my calling, Clay. Maybe I should take up stage acting. Personally, I never figured you'd fall for it, but from the look on your face, I reckon you did."

Slowly, like the rising of the sun, I began to understand the deception he had played on me. "You mean—"

"Yep. And it worked slicker than a greased cattle rope."

From behind, Bill spoke up, alarm evident in her voice. "Clay. Who is he? What's going on?"

I kept my eyes fixed on Joe. Sarcasm laced my reply. "My friend, Joe Sterling. The one who got himself shot and killed back in Kansas City." I paused, then added, "He figured that way I'd stop worrying about him."

"Worrying about him for what?"

"Guess."

She gasped.

Beside me, Twitch loosed a stream of tobacco onto the ground.

Joe chuckled at the obvious slight. "Sticks and stones, Twitch. Sticks and stones." With slow deliberation, he shucked his six-gun and held it centered on my midsection. "Now, old friend. I reckon you know what I want. Time to unload that wagon."

Bill screamed. "Clay!"

"Quiet." I demanded. "You won't get away with it, Joe." I dropped my right hand slowly.

A sneer twisted his lips, and his cold eyes flicked down to my hand. "I've already gotten away with it." He gestured to the hardcases behind him with the muzzle of his six-gun. "Wouldn't you say so?"

Keeping my eyes on Joe, I muttered to Twitch. "Move aside, Twitch."

My old partner jerked his head around at me in shock. "Clay! You ain't got a chance."

Joe spoke up in a soft, chilling voice. "He's right, Clay. Don't touch that hogleg. Even if I was to give you a fair break, which I ain't, I'm still too fast for you. The gold ain't yours anyway."

I stared hard at him. If I was going to make a play, then now was—

He must have read my intention in my eyes. Before I could finish my thought, his six-gun spat out an orange flame. A powerful blow slammed into my left shoulder, knocking me out of the saddle.

Bill and Louisa screamed.

I was told later that Timmy charged Joe with his horse, but Joe just laughed and frightened the horse so that it pawed at the air, and Timmy slid off his back.

Moments later, hands were on my shoulder, ripping away my shirt. I was too stunned to make much sense of the next few seconds, but I realized it was Bill trying to stop the bleeding. Then the table crashed to the ground, and the splitting of wood cut through the fuzziness in my head.

I fumbled for my Colt, but a boot heel clamped down on my wrist, pressing my hand into the ground.

Joe leered down at me. "Don't try it, Clay. I don't want to shoot you again."

"You get your foot off him, you-you—" Bill shouted, leaning over me and slapping ineffectually at his boot.

He laughed. "She's got spirit, Clay. I'll give her that."

Beyond Bill, two of the hardcases filled two saddlebags with the gold coins.

Joe squatted and picked up my Colt. He gestured to one of his men who wore a bushy beard. "Shorty. Take up their guns. Then carry them out to the middle of the river and toss 'em in the water." He removed his boot heel from my wrist. "Can't leave you with no guns, but by the time you get them and reload, we'll be a good piece from here.

Bill had helped me to lean up against a wagon wheel. I glared at Joe. "It isn't over. I'll find you."

He sneered. "I reckon you're stubborn enough that you'll blasted well try, but you best make it fast or there won't be any of the gold left." He glanced at the owlhoots filling the bags. "Hurry it up, Boys. Fort Worth and the gals are expecting us."

Bill worked quickly on my shoulder, placing a pad on either side. Luckily the slug caught the fleshy part of my shoulder below the collarbone. It hurt like the blazes, but as far as I could tell, nothing was broken.

Joe's man returned from the river. "They're taking a nice cold bath, Boss."

For a brief moment, Joe smiled sadly at me. "Hate to do that to the Colt, Clay. But, it'll clean up." He looked around. "All right, boys, let's don't waste no more time." He wheeled his pony about and touched his fingers to the brim of his hat. "So long, Clay," he said, spurring his horse to the south.

Twitch climbed on his horse. "Sunny, get Clay in the wagon and head for that stand of oak yonder. Boil some water. I'll fetch our guns."

Within minutes, water boiled rapidly on a hot fire blazing in the middle of the oaks. Gently, Bill bathed my shoulder in hot water, then opened the bottle of medicinal whiskey. "This is going to sting." I nodded, and she poured. She was right. The whiskey did sting. After wrapping my shoulder, she rummaged through my saddlebags for another shirt. Then she slid my arm in a sling she had tied around my neck.

"Here. Chew this." Sunny handed me a petal of peyote. I had used the medicine often in the past, both for myself and others. An Indian remedy, it was just as effective as laudanum but not as addictive.

While we were nooning, clouds rolled in from the south. At first I cursed when I spotted them, but then I realized it was a stroke of luck. Sign was next to impossible to track in dry sand, but rain would firm up the sand, leaving clear sign.

"Got some weather coming," Twitch drawled. "I reckon if it's not one thing going wrong, it's something else."

Sunny pointed at the broken table. "I best take the wagon and pick up your table, Ma'am."

"I'll go help," Timmy offered.

"Me too," Bill climbed in the wagon. "Not that there is too much to save."

With a shrug, Twitch climbed on his horse, and followed the wagon. "Might as well help. Don't reckon much more can go wrong."

The wind picked up ahead of the dark, churning clouds that marched ominously in our direction. The entire horizon was black, and lightning lanced from the heavens, spearing the ground with brilliant white slashes of light accompanied by booming drumbeats of thunder.

I watched helplessly as Sunny and Twitch tethered the horses. They had rigged a fly with two sides from the wagon to nearby trees. The open side faced away from the rapidly approaching storm.

The storm struck with a vengeance. Despite the stand of oaks breaking the wind and driving rain, water found its way through the seams of the shelter. Soon the ground was soaked except for the fire bed, which Sunny had the foresight to raise and then dig a small trench to funnel the water around.

Grimacing against the throbbing in my shoulder, I leaned back against the wagon wheel and closed my eyes against the pain.

Bill knelt at my side. "How are you doing?"

I nodded. "Reckon as well as could be expected."

She held the canteen to my lips. "Here. Drink. Sunny's putting supper on. You'll feel better after you eat."

While I had no appetite, I forced myself to eat to build up my strength. I figured on riding out next morning on Joe Sterling's trail, a plan I confided to no one.

During supper, the wind slacked, and the rain

slowed to a drizzle, one I guessed would last all night. Soon, the combination of a full belly, a warm fire, and another petal of peyote put me to sleep.

The slow drizzle was still falling when I awakened early the next morning. To my surprise, Bill was sleeping on a tarp spread on the ground next to me. Twitch and Sunny squatted by the small fire sipping coffee. A Bull Durham dangled from Sunny's lips.

Twitch spotted me and loosed a squirt of tobacco on the still wet ground. "You sure slept like a baby, Partner. I never seen a man sawing logs like you was doing."

I grimaced when I moved my shoulder. I expected some pain, but not the intense pain shooting through my shoulder. Sunny poured me a cup of six-shooter coffee. "Here. Don't move around. You'll start up the bleeding again."

"Thanks," I muttered, gratefully leaning back against the wagon wheel. The coffee warmed my belly. "Good."

At that moment, Bill stirred.

Twitch drawled. "She looked after you all night. Reckon you might be kind of special to her, huh?" He grinned mischievously.

"Not hardly," I replied.

She sat up, rubbed the sleep from her eyes, and looked at me, surprised I was sitting up and seemed fairly pert. "How do you feel this morning?"

I chuckled. "I don't reckon I could take on a bag of wildcats, but I'll live."

Twitch and Sunny grinned.

Bill crawled to me and unbuttoned my shirt, sliding it off my shoulder. She raised the bandage to inspect the wound. "Any hot water?" She spoke over her shoulder.

"Yes, Ma'am," Sunny replied.

Then, very briskly and methodically, Bill removed my bandages, bathed the wound with water hot enough to blister, then doused it with whiskey.

Twitch cringed. "Lordy, Lordy. Sure hate to see that," he muttered, turning his head and directing a stream of tobacco from the shelter onto the muddy ground. "A pure waste of good whiskey."

"Don't argue with her, Twitch. The sooner she gets me over this, the sooner I get on Joe Sterling's trail."

Bill froze, her fingers holding the clean bandage to my shoulder. She stared at me in disbelief. "You're not going anywhere for a week."

I gave her a crooked grin. I nodded to the drizzle outside. "I'm pulling out as soon as that stops."

"You can't," she replied, a hint of pleading in her voice. "You'll start up the bleeding again." She hesitated, reading the look of determination in my eyes. "You really mean that, don't you?"

"Reckon so."

Her eyes flashing fire, she leaped to her feet and threw the bandage at me. "If you don't have any better sense than that, then I'm not going to waste my time on you. You can just take care of yourself."

She spun on her heel and snapped at Sunny. "Where's a cup?"

Meekly, he handed her one. She poured too fast. The cup overflowed and spilled onto the fire. I couldn't make out what she muttered, but I had the feeling I was just as well off not knowing.

She slammed the pot back into the coals and stood staring into the rain, her back to me.

Chapter Fifteen

Intimidated by Bill's sharp and sudden burst of anger, neither Twitch nor Sunny uttered a word. I sat my coffee on the ground and fumbled with the bandage, refolding it and placing it on my shoulder.

Twitch glanced at Bill, then cleared his throat. "Want me to help you with that, Clay?"

I glanced at her rigid back. "Reckon so. I can hold this one in front, but I need three hands to do it all by myself."

Abruptly, Bill spun and glared down at me. She slung her coffee on the fire and threw her cup to the ground. "Here. I'll do it. I shouldn't, but you two would make such a mess, it would be worse than no bandage at all." She knelt at my side and slapped my hand away from my shoulder.

Her face was right close to mine as she worked. I looked at her. I hadn't really noticed, but she was right pretty even when she was angry. She glanced up at me, and I quickly looked away, staring at the canvas roof over my head, for some reason embarrassed she had caught me watching her.

Mid-afternoon, the rain ceased. Bill kept her eyes deliberately averted. Using my good arm, I hoisted myself to my feet by holding onto the rim of the wagon wheel. I stood for a moment, my legs unsteady. Suddenly, a wave of dizziness swept over me, and I had to wrap my arm around the rim to keep from falling.

"Clay!" Twitch called out.

I shook my head. "I'm okay. Just a little dizzy," I replied, easing my lanky carcass back to the ground. I dragged my tongue across my dry lips. "I don't suppose I'm as pert as I thought."

"I told you so," Bill said sharply, still keeping her eyes averted.

Leaning back against the wheel, I closed my eyes, too weary to argue. "Yes, Ma'am. I reckon you did."

Twitch drawled. "Suppose we might as well spend another night. Too late to start up today."

I didn't argue with him either.

While the gunshot wound had completely taken away any appetite I might have had, I still forced myself to put myself around some biscuits and gravy Sunny had whipped up.

I was smoking an after supper cigarette when Timmy and Louisa came to my side. I grinned at them. "You staying dry?" I asked with a weak laugh.

"Not too much," Timmy said.

Louisa spoke in a tiny voice, her eyes on my shoulder. "Does it hurt much?"

"Nope." Silently, I thanked the numbing effects of the peyote. I looked at Timmy. "I heard you tried to help me out yesterday. That was a brave thing you did running your horse at the man. You could have been hurt."

The boy grinned sheepishly, "He made me mad for what he did to you."

I nodded. "Well, I thank you. I thank you both."

Later that night as I lay staring at the shadows dancing on the canvas roof, I couldn't help thinking about the youngsters and the change that our journey had brought about. For whatever reason, Louisa chattered like a little squirrel now, and Timmy—well, he seemed to have gone through a complete turnaround from the spoiled brat stepping off the train. The only question still festering in my mind was the twenty dollar gold piece he had offered Rafe Abernathy to take care of me back in Baxter Springs.

I truly hoped the coin was his. I glanced toward the wagon, reluctant to ask him about the double eagle.

Next morning, I felt much better. Around the fire, we discussed the possible destinations of Joe Sterling and his cronies.

Twitch drawled. "If they go to Fort Worth like Joe said, they'll probably stop off in Paris first."

Bill frowned. "Paris?"

"Texas, Ma'am," Twitch explained. "About thirty miles or so southwest of us."

"There's no telling," I replied. "Honey Grove and Bonham is west, Shockey is east. The last thing I'll believe about Joe Sterling now is what he says, the lying no-account. He said Fort Worth, which means he won't go south." I watched Bill from the corner of my eyes as I continued. "I'd planned on following, but two days now of this rain, I'd never find their trail. I reckon it's best we get on home. From there, I'll run that polecat down."

We pulled out thirty minutes later, figuring if I couldn't stand the saddle, I'd ride in the wagon. After the first couple hours, I was feeling better, having adjusted to riding with one arm in a sling. Still, I was mighty glad to see noon so I could take a break from the jarring of my horse.

The afternoon was easier. My wound had not broken open, and I was handling the jarring better than I had during the morning spell.

Just before sundown, we decided to camp in a motte of scrub oak surrounding a rocky outcrop the size of a barn. Twitch rode ahead. He reined up and held up his hand. I rode up beside him. "What's wrong?"

He shook his head. "Nothing, I don't suppose. It's just that someone camped here during the storm." Before us was a clearing with the remains of a campfire well back under a rocky ledge. Empty whiskey bottles littered the ground.

We exchanged knowing glances. "You reckon it could be?" Twitch drawled.

"It could be," I announced, pulling up and nodding toward several sets of horse tracks leading east out of the scrub. "Take a look. I make five or six. About a day or so old."

He grunted. "Looks like." He rode ahead, winding his way through the scrub oak as he followed the trail. He reined up at the edge of the motte and pointed east to a column of circling buzzards.

I pulled up. The squeak of leather against leather was the only sound as I shifted in the saddle to peer in the direction he was pointing. "Could be wolves pulled down a deer." Then I thought about Joe Sterling. "Maybe something else," I added.

Twitch caught the nuance in my tone. "What's on your mind?"

I rode back to where the wagon had pulled up in the clearing. "We'll camp here. Twitch and me spotted a heap of buzzards back to the east. We're going to take a look at what's got those buzzards so interested."

"Can I go?"

I looked around at Timmy sitting astride his pony. "I reckon so. Just stay behind us when we get close over yonder."

He nodded. "Yes, Sir."

Twitch was a few hundred yards ahead of us. I couldn't help noticing the trail we had followed through the scrub led directly to the circling buzzards.

As Twitch drew near the buzzards, a dozen more

lumbered into the air. They were thicker than horse flies in May. He reined up and remained in his saddle. I frowned as I drew near. Twitch hadn't moved. He was sitting motionless in his saddle staring at the ground in front of him.

I had been partially right. The wolves had been busy as had the buzzards, but not on deer. Sprawled on the prairie in front of us lay four dead cowboys, their carcasses worked over by the varmints so that not even a mother could have recognized her own son.

They weren't too ripe, although the stench of the exposed entrails and other offal lay heavily over the scene. Behind me, Timmy gagged.

Twitch rolled his tobacco in his cheek and squirted an arc through the air. "You figure the same as me?"

"Yep." I nodded, my eyes fixed on the carnage before us. "Whoever they were, they're the ones we followed from the clearing."

A movement caught my eye. I glanced up to see a wolf vanish into the sage. Then I spotted another one.

"What do you mean, whoever they was? You know who they was. Those were the hardcases with Joe Sterling."

By now, dusk had crept over the prairie, and at the same time, half-a-dozen lobos started creeping back toward their disturbed meals.

I reined around. "Too dark to get a handle on the others tonight. We'll take a look at first light."

After telling the others of our discovery, I caught Bill looking at me with a wry smile on her face. When she realized I had noticed her, she shook her head. "I suppose you're going after them in the morning." There was a touch of acceptance in her voice.

"No choice. There's two left."

Twitch guffawed. "If I know Joe Sterling, there ain't but one now."

He was probably right.

Her eyes dropped to my shoulder. In a resigned voice, she said. "Well, at least I got you to rest it for a couple days. I suppose that's better than nothing." She drew a deep breath, then released it. "I'll bandage it again before you leave in the morning."

I grinned at her. "Thanks."

Around the campfire that night, we laid out our plans for the coming days. "You remember how to get home, don't you, Twitch?" I grinned at him.

He snorted. " 'Course I do. I could take these folks down there blindfolded."

Despite his assurances, I went over the directions once again. "Remember, head southeast for Fort Sherman in Hopkins County, then on down to Chilton in Upshur County. There's a ferry over the Sabine River there. Afterwards, its about two days due south to the Angelina. Then follow it on to the ranch. I'll catch up with you somewhere along the trail."

Twitch looked at Sunny with a pained expression on his face. "This young feller's clucking like a pullet to an old rooster."

Sunny laughed. "Be patient with him, Twitch. He's still wet behind the ears."

Bill ignored their sarcasm. "Where are you heading first?"

I pondered the question. "Can't say. All I know for sure is, in the morning, I'll pick up their trail and tag along to wherever it leads."

She drew a deep breath. I could see the consternation in her eyes. For some strange reason, I had the overwhelming urge to still her fears.

"First, understand something." I nodded to my grizzled partner. "Twitch there will be first to tell you I can't take Joe in a showdown. But, he'll also tell you, I'm not dumb enough to try. When I make my play, and I will, I'll have all the advantages. Joe Sterling is too good to give a chance."

I figured my little show of bravado did what I intended, for a faint smile played over her lips. "I hope so," she replied. "I hope so."

"Me, too," Timmy chimed in.

"And me, too," Louisa added.

Chapter Sixteen

Next morning after breakfast while we were saddling our ponies, I glanced at Timmy. He was tightening the cinch on his saddle just like an old hand. Twitch was busy checking his horse's hooves, so I decided this was the time to return the double eagle I'd been carrying in my pocket ever since Baxter Springs.

"Here you go, Timmy," I said, flipping him the coin. "This is yours."

He caught the double eagle deftly and stared down at it.

When I saw his ears redden, I knew he had taken the coin from the table. He looked up at me slowly, almost reluctantly, and I explained. "I got it from the cowboy you gave it to."

The color on his face deepened. "I—" He bit his bottom lip.

"Look, Timmy. I don't know if it's yours or not. You gave it to Rafe, he gave it to me, and I'm returning it."

He swallowed hard. "But, what do I do with it?"

I studied him a moment. "You've growed up a heap since you got off the train up in Kansas City. I reckon you can figure out what to do."

Before Timmy could reply, Twitch dropped his horse's foot. "Thought it was bruised. It ain't."

Timmy cut his eyes toward Twitch, then looked back at me. He slipped the coin into his pocket and turned away.

We parted ways ten minutes later. The others headed south. I headed east, filled with a strange mixture of regret and excitement. As I climbed the small rise overlooking the dead cowpokes, I cast one last look back at the wagon in time to see it disappear over the crest of a hill to the south. Often I had traveled alone, but now for the first time, an alien sense of loneliness flooded over me.

When I reached the top of the rise, the fetid odor of decomposing flesh hit me full in the face along with the squawk of startled buzzards and the guttural snarl of frightened wolves. I pressed my lips together and tried to close my throat. There were only two of the cowpokes left. Wolves and coyotes had dragged the others into the sage, but from the remains of the two cowpokes below, the varmints had done their usual thorough job.

All I could do was shake my head.

I circled the site and cut the trail to the east

One of the horses' tracks sank deeper in the still damp sand than the other. Joe's, I figured. Naturally, he would be the one carrying the gold. "What do you want to bet, Horse, that each one of those no-account jaspers is watching the other like a hawk?"

A faint chuckle rolled off my lips as I pictured the two of them in my head, one eye on the trail, the other on his partner, and their hands never far from the butt of their six-guns.

Travel long enough under that tension, something would explode. Maybe I'd get lucky, and the two would shoot it out. Who knows, I told myself. I might run across them both lying dead on the other side of yonder hill.

I didn't, but I did stay on their trail, and it led straight to Paris, the crossroads of northeast Texas.

The small town had a single street, lined with an odd collection of buildings constructed from every imaginable material. Most were of logs, some of canvas with false fronts, and two or three of hand-sawn board and batten.

Several horses stood hipshot at the hitching rails in the mud. A freight wagon was parked in front of the general store, while a whiskey wagon delivered its goods to one of the several saloons in the town.

Along the boardwalks lounged cowpokes as well as townsfolk.

I knew Joe wouldn't bushwhack me on the street. He wouldn't have to. He could outdraw and outshoot me, and he knew it. On the other hand, I wasn't about to give his compadre the chance. I pulled the brim of my John B. down over my eyes and slumped back in the saddle as I amble into town.

A few eyes glanced at me, then dismissed me as a drifter. Without looking left or right, I pulled up in front of the Gay Paree Saloon and dismounted.

The tinny sounds of a piano came through the batwing doors. I pushed them aside and headed for the bar that stretched along one wall. I ordered a ten-cent beer, which allowed me my fill from the coldcut and condiment table where I built me a thick sandwich.

Then I found a empty spot at the end of the bar and waited and watched, making certain I kept my head down and peering along the bar from beneath the brim of my hat. I knew I probably could not recognize Joe's partner right off, but I could recognize a twenty dollar gold piece.

Before closing time, I made four more bars with no luck.

My arm was throbbing. Despite the fact the four beers were having their way with me, my shoulder throbbed, so I popped in another petal of peyote and decided to find a spot to rest my weary bones. I put my horse in the livery.

Back outside, I stopped a local gent and inquired about a place for the night.

He looked me up and down, then pointed to a two-story clapboard across the street. "Over there at Red Dot Hotel. They'll take care of you for the night. Two dollars. Go up the side stairs and ask for Mary. Tell her Fargo sent you."

I frowned. "Reckon rooms are hard to find around here, huh?"

He gave me a sly grin. "Good ones."

I followed his directions, puzzling over his instructions to give her his name. But then, I figured that maybe he received a commission on the number of customers he sent the hotel.

The lobby upstairs was gaudy with heavy red drapes from which dangled gold tassels. It was a little too fancy for me, and I was about to head back to the livery and a bed of straw when a plump, middle-aged woman swept into the room and greeted me.

"Welcome, Cowboy. What can I do for you?" She wore heavy makeup, and her hair hung down in ringlets about her shoulders. She looked me squarely in the eye.

I decided to play out my hand. "Just a room for the night, Ma'am. A gent by the name of Fargo sent me. Said I was to see Mary."

She eyed my arm in a sling, and then a broad smile played over her face. "I'm Mary, and I'll fix you right up. You look like a gent who knows what he wants. You've come to the right place." She held out her hand. "That'll be two dollars."

She acted like she was trying to sell me something, but, I pushed the feeling aside. All I wanted was a hotel room. I paid her, and she led the way upstairs and to the front. "Last one on the left, Cowboy. All the rest are in use." She looked around and grinned wickedly. "Good use."

"Thanks," I replied, puzzled at her remark, "good use" I shrugged it off when she lit the lamp in the room. The bed was mighty inviting.

She paused before closing the door. "Enjoy yourself," she said with the big smile still on her face. "Anything you don't like, let me know. We aim to please."

Still puzzled, I nodded. She was certainly a friendly hotel owner. "Yes, Ma'am. I'll do that."

When she closed the door, I shucked my clothes down to my long johns and plopped down on the bed. I sprawled out on the bed and sighed contentedly as my sore muscles relaxed.

Without warning, the door opened, and a young woman wearing a black negligee that didn't hide much of anything waltzed in, her coal black hair framing a heart-shaped face wearing a big smile.

With a sultry look in her eyes and a husky rasp to her voice, she said, "Hello there, Cowboy. My name's Colette, and I'm yours for the night."

Instinctively, I yanked the sheet up to my neck. All I could do was stammer.

She sat on the edge of the bed and caressed my cheek. "There, there. Don't be nervous. I won't bite." She smiled gently as if she had soothed the nervousness of many a young man.

Finally, words tumbled from my lips. "Excuse me, ah-Colette-Ma'am, but there's been some mistake here, I think."

Her slender fingers ceased their ministrations of my cheek. A tiny frown wrinkled her forehead. "But, you paid for me for the night."

"No, Ma'am." I shook my head. "Well, at least, I didn't mean to—no offense intended. I just wanted a room for the night—to sleep," I added. "I—I didn't know this was—well. . . ."

Her frown deepened. She began to pout.

I hated it when women pouted, so I hastened to explain. "Of course, if I had in mind what you thought I had in mind, I'll certainly be right happy to spend my time with you. But, I didn't have in mind what you thought I had in mind." I frowned, not quite certain I had said what I meant to say.

I must have for the smile returned to her face. "Really? You'd pick me?"

I nodded. "Really." I studied her a moment, trying to guess her age. She couldn't even be twenty.

Colette glanced around at the door, then turned back to me. A frown wrinkled her forehead. "I don't know what I'm going to do. I can't leave. Mary will fire me, and I need the money. When I save enough, I'm going to Denver and take singing lessons."

By now, I had scooted into a sitting position, leaning against the headboard. The sheet was still drawn up about my neck. "Well, now. I wouldn't want her to fire you." Reluctantly, I said. "I suppose you could stay here."

Her eyes lit. "You mean, share the bed?"

Quickly, I set her straight. "No. I'll take the sheet and sleep on the floor. You take the bed."

She frowned, and I had the feeling I had made a smart move by taking the floor. It wasn't that she couldn't trust me. It was the other way around. I didn't think I could trust her.

She blew out the lamp. I heard the bedsprings squeak as she lay down. Staring into the dark above my head. In a thin voice, she said, "What's your name, Cowboy?"

Staring into the darkness above my head, I replied, "Clay—Clay Morgan."

Almost apologetically, she continued, "My real name isn't Colette, you know. Mary said it sounded French, and that men liked French ladies. My real name is Alwilda."

"Alwilda. Why, that's a right pretty name."

"You really think so?"

I felt sorry for the kid. She desperately wanted folks to approve of her. With the exception of my Pa and the ranch hands, I had never really cared one way or another what folks thought. I supposed it was sort of jarring to realize that there were folks out there like Alwilda who were desperate for approval. "Yes, Alwilda is a mighty pretty name."

We grew silent. I tried to imagine what her life was like, and then an idea struck me. "Colette—I mean, Alwilda. Has anyone come in here the last couple days spending twenty-dollar gold pieces?"

Her disembodied voice came from the darkness. "Not that I know—wait. Yes, there was. Yesterday. He wasn't one of mine. I was glad. He had a heavy beard, and I don't like men with beards. He was Patricia's. She said he had a pocketful of gold coins."

That had to be the owlhoot that helped Joe kill the others. I tried to still the excitement in my voice. "Was he by himself. I mean, did his partner come in with him?"

"She didn't say. All he told her was he was pulling out the next morning for Maple Springs over in Red River County."

By now, sleep was the last thing on my mind.

"Light the lamp, Alwilda."

"But why?"

"Just light it."

She did as I asked and watched in surprise as I quickly dressed, which was a clumsy task with one hand.

"Where are you going?"

"Leaving," I said, buckling on my gunbelt.

She looked frantically at the door. "But, if Mary sees you, she'll fire me. I can't afford to lose this job."

I looked around at her in frustration. "Okay. I don't want you to lose your job. So, I'll go out the window." I fished in my pocket and handed her five dollars. "Maybe this will help with those singing lessons."

She nodded and smiled at me. "You are a true gentleman, Sir."

"Some folks would disagree," I replied, thinking of Bill.

After raising the window, I climbed out on the balcony overlooking the street. Parked below was a whiskey wagon loaded with barrels. The top row of

wooden barrels was only about six feet below the balcony. All I had to do was climb over the railing and
drop to the barrels—with one arm in a sling.

Simple.

I swung first one leg over the railing, then the other,
all the while hanging on for dear life with one hand.
Finally, I balanced myself on the edge. Then, clutch-
ing the railing, I leaned back and stared down between
my legs at the barrels, which now appeared to be a
quarter-of-a-mile beneath me instead of the original
six feet. I took aim at the last barrel on the top row.

Taking a deep breath, I pushed back and dropped
on the barrels. I landed squarely, the way I planned,
but the barrel slammed down between the barrels on
the bottom row, causing three of them to squirt out
the rear of the wagon and smash into pieces on the
ground, spilling almost five hundred gallons of whiskey.

Off balance, I followed them to the ground, landing
in the middle of the five hundred gallons of whiskey
and mud. Without hesitation, I jumped to my feet and
raced to the livery.

I wasted no time saddling my pony and heading out
the back door of the livery for Maple Springs in Red
River County.

Chapter Seventeen

Maple Springs was a third the size of Paris, which made my search much easier, so easy in fact that I found my man in the first saloon.

I was standing at the end of the bar when I spotted the twenty dollar gold piece roll across the wet surface. A gravelly voice echoed down the bar. "Gimme a bottle, Bartender. Your best."

I shot a glance from under the brim of my hat at the speaker. It was Shorty, the cowpoke who had dumped our guns in the river. I lowered my head, and slowly turned my back on him. I didn't want to chance being recognized, so instead of leaving by the front door, which meant I would have to pass directly behind him, I headed out the back already formulating a plan.

Across the street, I stopped in the general store for a can of peaches, which I promptly placed in my saddlebag until I needed them. Then I plopped down on the wooden bench in front of the general store and waited.

I didn't have long.

Thirty minutes later, Shorty staggered from the bar, fished in his saddlebags, then stumbled back inside. Looked to me he was figuring on a night of bucking the tiger.

My stomach growled. Two doors down, the cheerful glow of lights from a café beckoned. Inside, I put myself around a thick steak and pot of coffee, all the while keeping my eyes on the saloon.

The Regulator clock chimed ten. I figured it was time to make my move. Shorty was still in the bar, so I ambled across the street and took up a spot between the batwing doors and front window. I needed to be close by when he came out for what I had in mind.

By one o'clock, the saloon was almost empty. From time to time, I glanced through the window. Shorty was still at the bar. Finally, he turned to leave. I hoped no one left with him.

Quickly, I surveyed the silent town. For what I planned, I needed at least ten seconds with no witnesses. I glanced one last time through the window. Shorty was almost to the door, but to my consternation, a second patron had shoved away from the bar and staggered for the door.

Hastily, I pressed up to the wall next to the door. I shucked my six-gun. Shorty stumbled out, letting the doors swing behind him. "Hey, Partner," I whispered.

"Huh?" He started to turn to me, but he never made

it for I cold-cocked him with the muzzle of my revolver. He slumped to the boardwalk. I quickly holstered my gun and knelt by his side just as the bar patron stepped through the doors. He jerked to a halt and stared down at me and Shorty. He swayed unsteadily on his feet and chuckled. "Couldn't handle the whiskey, huh? I told him he was knocking them drinks down too fast."

I grinned up at him. "Reckon so. I've told him that too. Do me a favor, Pard. I got me a bad arm. Help me throw him over his saddle. I'll see he gets to bed."

After tossing the unconscious cowpoke over his saddle and lashing his feet to his hands under his pony's belly, I calmly swung onto my own mount and headed out of town.

When he awakened next morning, Shorty was seated on the leaf- and pine needle-carpeted ground, lashed to a thick pine. I had removed his trousers. A few seconds passed before his situation dawned on him. He blinked once or twice, then shook his head. "Hey! What's going on here? Who are you?" He paused a moment, glanced at his long johns, then demanded. "Where's my pants?"

I was squatting by the small fire sipping a cup of coffee. I pointed to his trousers at my side. "Right here, Shorty."

He frowned. "How'd you know my name? Who are you?"

"Why wouldn't I know the name of the hombre who robbed me of twenty-five thousand dollars in gold?"

His face paled, and his eyes grew wide with recognition. He looked at my arm in the sling, then stammered, "Y-You're the jasper that Joe shot."

"If we were back in the bar, I'd buy you a drink for being so smart, Shorty."

"What do you want with me?" His eyes darted from side to side, looking for some way out of his predicament.

"Forget it, Shorty. No one's coming to help. In fact, nobody knows where you are except me, so if you want to get out of this with all your skin, you'll tell me one thing."

"Yeah. What?"

"Where is Joe Sterling?"

He snorted. "I ain't telling you nothing."

I shook my head. "Bad choice, Shorty, but then, seeing the sort of vermin you run with, I reckon you're given to making bad choices." I slowly poured the remainder of my coffee on the fire, then rose to my feet. Moving deliberately, I pulled my knife from its sheath and started toward the struggling cowpoke.

"What are you going to do?" His eyes widened in alarm.

"Don't worry, I'm not going to kill you, but before I'm finished, you'll wish you were."

He caught his breath when I walked past him. I retrieved the can of peaches from my saddlebag and squatted in front of him. "I always had a hankering for peaches," I told him, at the same time cutting open the top of the can. "Yes, sir, they sure do hit the spot," I added, spearing a chunk and popping it in my mouth.

"Sure do wish you'd tell me what I want to know. Make it a heap easier on yourself."

He glared defiantly at me and jerked unsuccessfully at the ropes binding him. "I ain't telling you nothing."

I ate another peach, lazily rose to my feet, and wandered down between two pines to a rotting hickory stump. Tilting the can, I poured some peach juice on the tub-sized bed of red ants on one side of the stump.

Casually, I sauntered back to Shorty, pouring out a continuous stream of juice.

His eyes grew wide. "What are you doing?"

I paused to eat another peach and shook my head. "I figured you were dumb, Shorty, but not that dumb."

"What?"

With a shrug, I continued pouring until I was within a few feet of him. I sat the can on the leafy ground, balanced my knife on top of it, picked up two pieces of rope, and lashed one about each of his ankles. I tied the other ends to separate trees, spreading his legs in a V.

Retrieving my knife, I knelt at his side. "Now, don't you start squirming about, Shorty. I only got one hand to use, and I'm still weak from this gunshot wound. I don't want to cut you."

He struggled against the ropes, his eyes wide with fear. Deftly I sliced the long johns around his leg about eight inches above his knee. Then I split them lengthwise to the ankle, folding them away from his legs, leaving them bare, white, and hairy.

I picked up the peach can. "You sure you won't tell me where Joe went?"

He shook his head jerkily.

"Too bad." I clucked, spearing another peach and then continuing the trail of peach juice. When I reached Shorty, I ran the trail of peach juice up one leg and back down another.

Then I sat back to wait.

Within minutes, the first red ant appeared, followed by a thick line of the savage little critters.

Shorty pleaded. "Hey, you can't do this. This ain't right."

"Neither was stealing the gold." I nonchalantly speared the last peach and poured the remainder of the juice on the leaves between his legs.

Then the first ants climbed up on his ankle. He squirmed and twisted, trying to throw them off, but more followed. Shorty groaned between clenched teeth. His groans turned into shouts of pain when the ants began biting him.

"Ouch, ow, ow, this is killing me," he screamed.

Casually, I said, "I hear some folks is allergic to ant bites. Too many, and they drop deader than a can of corned beef. Now are you going to tell me where Joe is?"

He might have held out a few more seconds, but a two-inch, green beetle with antennae curved like one of those Arabian swords started up his thigh.

Shorty screamed, a blood-chilling shriek that echoed through the forest. "Fulton! He's going to Fulton on the Red over in Arkansas."

I remained in a squat. "You're not lying to me now, are you Shorty?"

Tears streamed down his cheeks. He shook his head. "No, no, I ain't. Please get them off me, please."

"Because if you are, I promise I'll come back and finish the job."

"I ain't lying. I ain't lying. I ain't lying."

I was even beginning to hurt for him, so I leaned over and slashed his legs free, then sliced the knot behind the tree. "Your pony's tied yonder behind you. I took the gold from your saddlebags. A smart man would leave the country."

Shorty didn't answer. He was too busy jumping to his feet, screaming and dancing around like a wild Indian and slapping at the ants climbing his legs.

I swung into the saddle and headed east. I'd never been to Fulton, but I figured I could find it.

By sundown, I reached Moorville. From the few inquiries at the local watering holes, I learned that Joe was only a day ahead of me. My stomach was beginning to knot. I had no idea how I was going to take him.

The liveryman told me to ride a few miles north to the Red River, and I could follow it right into Fulton.

I wondered how much of the twenty-five thousand Joe had left. I'd taken a little over four from Shorty. With a wry laugh, I muttered, "You sure aren't much of a businessman, Shorty. He gets twenty and you get five."

By the time I camped at sundown outside of Fulton the next day, I knew I had to take Joe by surprise. I had no stomach for killing, but I was determined to take back the money.

The only problem with my plan was that I didn't know just how I would surprise him. "We'll just have to wait and see what comes up," I mumbled, rolling out my soogan and drawing the blanket up to my chest.

I didn't sleep much that night. I just hoped that by this time the next day, I would still be alive.

Chapter Eighteen

Before riding into Fulton the next morning, I removed my sling. I wanted to appear nondescript, commonplace.

My arm was sore, but I figured I could work the soreness out.

I put my horse up at the livery and found a spot in the shade of a large oak just outside the livery. Pulling my hat brim down over my eyes, I pulled out my knife and started whittling.

Mid-morning, I spotted Joe coming out of the Lassiter Hotel and Food Emporium. He headed in my direction. My heart thudded against my chest. I leaned back and rested my chin on my chest, hoping I appeared to be sleeping.

His boots crunched on the ground, and then I heard the squeak of the livery door opening. *Was he riding out?*

Moments later, I had my answer. The door squeaked again, and Joe called out, "You done a good job with my horse, old man. Take good care of him. I'm riding out first thing in the morning."

I watched through slit eyes as he angled away from the hotel to the nearest bar. I looked back at the hotel. That's where the money was. I was certain. He wouldn't bury it, he wouldn't bank it, he wouldn't leave it in the livery. No, the money was in his room.

Mid-afternoon I visited the local tonsorial parlor for a shave, haircut, and bath, after which I donned fresh duds. Figuring I was now presentable, I headed to the hotel, planning on a meal in the Emporium. I wanted the staff to see me, grow accustomed to me so that they would think nothing amiss when I plopped down in one of the plush chairs in the lobby and went to sleep.

I kept my fingers crossed and my eyes moving. I didn't want to run into Joe before I could put my plan into play.

I got lucky. Joe remained in the saloon all afternoon. At six o'clock, he entered the hotel lobby. I feigned sleep and watched as he gave a young bellhop a greenback and pointed across the street. "And make sure it's good stuff."

Here was my chance.

After Joe climbed the stairs, I sauntered outside and waited for the boy to return. Moments later, he trotted across the street lugging a bottle of whiskey. I stopped him. "Hey, Son. What do you have there?"

He nodded upstairs and held up the bottle. "It's for the gent in 203."

I pulled out a twenty dollar gold piece. "He's a friend of mine. How about you letting me take it up to him?" I offered the boy the coin.

"You bet," he replied instantly, shoving the bottle at me and grabbing the coin.

Moments later, I knocked on the door to 203.

"Yeah?"

I raised the pitch of my voice. "It's me, Mister. I got the whiskey for you."

"Come in. Door's open. Put it on the dresser. I'm in the tub."

I couldn't believe my luck. With a drawn six-gun in one hand and the bottle in the other, I opened the door and shoved it wide open with my toe.

Joe had his back to me, vigorously scrubbing his shoulders with a long-handled brush while he hummed "Sweet Betsy from Pike." I sat the bottle down with a loud thud.

"Hey, Boy. Don't break—" He glanced around and his face went slack.

"Hello, Joe," I said casually, kicking the door closed with my heel and quickly crossing the room to his gunbelt hanging on the headboard.

For a moment, he started to rise, then sat back, a look of disgust on his face.

"I told you I'd find you."

A crooked grin played over his face. "Yep. I reckon you did. So now what?"

"So, now I'm taking the gold."

"What about me?"

"Won't do no good to turn you over to the law. They won't believe either one of us."

His grin grew cold. "You know I'll follow you. That's too much money for a country boy like you. I know how to use it. I can appreciate it."

"Don't do it, Joe. One of us might get killed. I sure don't want it to be me, and I'd hate for it to be you."

He laughed. "That was always your one failing, Clay. You don't have the stomach to kill."

"Makes no difference." I glanced around. "Now where's th—"

With an angry growl, he leaped from the tub at me. I took a quick step back and slammed my six-gun across the back of his head.

He collapsed like an empty flour sack.

Staring down at him, I muttered. "I should put a hole in you like you did me, Joe." But I couldn't. I was in a fine quandary. The law wouldn't lock him up. If it came to a shootout, he'd gun me down.

My brain raced. I needed time.

I managed to hoist him on the bed and tie him as tightly as I could with strips torn from the sheets and blankets. I gagged him, after which I searched the room for the gold.

Joe had stashed it in the bottom drawer of the dresser. I grabbed it and started for the door. Abruptly

I jerked to a halt. I couldn't help grinning. I needed every minute of time I could get.

Quickly, I collected his boots and clothes and gunbelt, and started to throw them out the window. I halted abruptly, staring at the Colt in his holster. I glanced down at mine, remembering when Joe gave it to me ten years earlier.

And now, he had played me wrong.

I stuck his Colt under my belt, then promptly tossed his gear out the window. Quickly, I unloaded my Colt and laid it on the dresser for him to see when he awakened. He was smart enough to figure out what the gesture meant. I dropped his in my holster. I glanced around at him one last time and shook my head.

My best bet was to hightail it out of Fulton, make for Texas, and hope to shake him from my tail.

That, I knew, would be harder than prying a turtle's jaws from your big toe.

I couldn't help chuckling as I hurried from the hotel door to the livery. The items I'd tossed out the window had already disappeared. By the time Joe awakened, straightened the whole mess out, I'd have a good twenty-four hours or more on him.

Then I had another idea.

The old liveryman looked on while I saddled up. I slung the saddlebags on behind the saddle and retrieved two gold coins. I offered them to the old man and pointed to Joe's black gelding. "Here's forty dollars to lose that animal for two days."

The old man's eyes glittered with greed. "Why?"

I shook my head. "You don't need to know. I just want the owner of that black to stay in town for two days.

"But, what do I say happened to the horse?"

"Say you don't know. You came in this morning, and the horse was gone. You figured he took it." I gestured down the street. "Tie the horse up outside of town somewhere."

The old man licked his lips and stared at the two gold coins.

"But if you're going to do it, you best do it now."

Without a word, he grabbed the coins, untied the black, and led it out the front door.

Quickly, I pulled out my knife and sliced the cinches on Joe's double-rigged saddle.

I rode all night, reaching the Sulphur River shortly before sunup. In the middle of the river, I turned my pony downstream and forced him to swim with the current several minutes before clambering ashore.

Directly south was the small town of Panther Flat, a mecca for every kind of owlhoot, and the last place I wanted to be seen. I cut east before reaching the small town, all the while keeping a close eye on the trail before and behind me. From time to time when I spotted a distant rider, I pulled off the trail and remained hidden until he passed, an easy task in the middle of the thick pine forests.

I avoided towns, stopping once at a farm on Cypress

Creek where I swapped my horse for a gray gelding with twenty dollars to boot.

"And I'd appreciate it, Friend," I said, "that you never saw me if any hombre should ask."

The farmer eyed the gold coin greedily. "Don't worry none, Mister. I ain't never laid eyes on you."

From his farm, I headed west toward Coffeeville, more than willing to ride extra miles in an effort to throw Joe off my trail. Then I cut south to Chilton, and from there, southeast, following the now familiar winding trace through the towering pines to Marion.

Two days later, I hit the headwaters of the Angelina River at the junction of Barnhardt and Shawnee creeks three miles northwest of Laneville. From there it flowed southeast for over a hundred miles to the Neches River. The Angelina water ran clear and sweet unlike the numerous rivers of mud carving through the red hills of East Texas.

My pony stumbled, then caught himself. I leaned forward and patted his neck. "Tired, huh, old boy? Me, too."

Pulling off the trail and up onto a rise overlooking the Angelina River, I decided to make an early camp that night. I had only another day and a half before reaching the Box D. I glanced over my back trail, my mind on Joe Sterling. Was he still on my trail? If so, where was he now? Maybe I should ride all night. As long as I had the gold with me, he was a danger. Once

I turned it over to Bill and her uncle, Hewitt Selby, I figured Joe would give up.

My horse shook his head and pulled at the reins.

I laughed and dismounted. "Why not?" I said to him. "We both deserve the rest. We'll pull out bright and early in the morning."

Chapter Nineteen

That night as I lay on my blankets, I wondered how J.R. and the children were taking to each other down at the Box D. And I thought about Bill. New faces meant changing times.

With a chuckle, I muttered to the silence around me. "Things won't ever be the same, J.R."

I awakened early the next morning to a typical East Texas morning. Shafts of sunlight slashed through the tall pines as the morning birds sang to the new day. I even whistled a tune as I sipped my coffee and bundled my gear.

Later, just as I finished tightening the saddle cinch on my gray, I spotted five jaspers on scrub ponies zigzagging through the pines up the hill toward me. Apparently, they'd spotted my smoke.

The hair on the back of my neck bristled. They were

a rough-looking bunch. I didn't cotton to them coming in too close. I reached over the saddle and slipped my Winchester from its boot.

"Howdy," I shouted.

They reined up some thirty yards distant.

One rode forward a couple steps. "Saw the smoke. Figured on some coffee."

"Sorry, Partner. I just put out the fire and was riding out."

He shook his head. "Sure do hate to hear that. Don't reckon you can spare any coffee grounds. We got a pot."

I shook my head. "Used the last this morning."

Even from this distance, I could see the leer on his bearded face. "Well, you ain't much help at all, are you?" He glanced over his shoulder. "Since he ain't got no coffee, Boys, maybe we just ought to take his horse."

Before he could say another word, I slapped my pony's rump and jumped behind a dead tree stump and squeezed off a shot. One of the jaspers in the rear screamed and tumbled from his horse. The others leaped to the ground and began firing.

"Go around, Luke. I'll keep him pinned down," one of the owlhoots shouted.

"I'll go the other way," another called out.

I grimaced. After all I'd been through, now a gang of hardcases were trying to finish what Joe had started. I chambered a round. They might finish it, but not all of them would be around afterward.

Taking a deep breath, I popped up over the top of

the stump and snapped off half-a-dozen shots then dropped back to one knee.

A slug tore off a chunk of wood at my feet. I spun and threw a shot at one cowpoke scrambling back behind a thick pine. He screamed. A boot popped out from behind the pine, and I promptly shot it.

The owlhoot screamed again.

A slug whizzed past my ear. I spun to the other side. They were closing in.

Suddenly, a shot rang out from behind me. I cringed. They had me surrounded, but to my surprise, one of the owlhoots leaped to his feet and sprawled face down on the ground.

That was three that had been hit. Two remained.

Then a familiar voice echoed through the forest. "You never can stay out of trouble, can you, Clay?"

Joe Sterling!

I snapped off another shot. "Seems that way," I yelled.

"How many left?"

"Two. In front of me."

"Pin them down. I'll swing around them."

"Hold on. Let me load up." Quickly I filled the magazine, then clacked one in the chamber. "All right. Say when."

"When!"

I jumped to my feet and sprayed the forest in front of me with lead plums. Slugs tore up the stump in front of me. From the corner of my eye, I glimpsed a black figure darting from tree to tree. The figure jerked, then disappeared behind a tree.

Slugs hummed past my ear, and then the sharp reports of Joe's Winchester echoed through the pine trees. For the next thirty seconds, the cacophony of gunfire bouncing off the pines reminded me of the fight for the Railroad Redoubt at the Battle of Vicksburg back in '63.

Abruptly, two jaspers took off running through the trees.

After a few moments, Joe called out. "Where are the others, Clay?"

"Two by you. One here by me."

He coughed. "Check yours. Be careful, though. Don't want nothing to happen to you."

As I drew closer to the one sprawled behind the tree, I called out. "Your compadres are either dead or running like scared rabbits. I don't cotton to shooting anyone, so you just get your carcass out of here."

"I can't," he whined. "My leg's busted."

"Then hop. You'll get no help from me. I'll let you keep your six-gun, but you fire one shot at me, you're dead. You understand?"

"Yeah."

I glanced at Joe who had his back to me. I resisted the urge to potshot him. I should have, but I couldn't although I knew why he was here. I took a deep breath and looked up at the clear sky.

After he inspected the second cowpoke, Joe turned back to me, a crooked grin on his face. His Winchester dangled at his side. "Lucky I came along, huh, Clay?" He started toward me and stumbled to his knees.

"Joe?"

He tried to laugh. "One of those galoots got me good and proper, Pard."

"Lord, Joe, no," I exclaimed, hurrying to him.

He shook his head slowly, "Afraid so," he mumbled, crumpling over on his side. "I don't believe it."

I knelt and lifted his shoulders, resting his head in the crook of my arm. "You crazy fool."

He grinned up at me, a trickle of blood oozing from the side of his lips. "I reckon I am, Pard. That's why I followed after you."

"The gold?"

He coughed. "What else?"

"Why didn't you let them do the job for you?"

He shook his head. "You never was too smart, Clay. You might have hid the gold. If they'd killed you, I'd never find it." Grimacing, he slipped his handgun from the holster. "You—You forgot this. You always was careless."

In his hand was my Colt. The early morning sun glittered on the double eagles inset in the handgrips.

Tears filled my eyes and my throat burned. "Hold on, Joe. I'll patch you best I can then get you to a sawbones."

"You was always the stubborn one, Clay. I never could learn you no better. Besides, cutting my cinch was a dirty trick." He raised his left hand. I clutched it with mine.

"Sorry about the saddle, Joe. Sorry about everything."

He squeezed my hand. And then he died.

* * *

I lost track of how long I sat holding Joe.

The whinny of a horse jerked me from my trance. The sun was directly overhead. Gently, I lowered Joe to the ground and retrieved our ponies.

Next day at mid-afternoon, I rode into the Box D.

We buried Joe in the ranch cemetery the next morning. Bill and her Uncle Hewitt Selby joined us.

Afterward, sitting on the covered porch, I related the details of my pursuit. When I finished, Louisa eased to my side and put her arms around my neck. "I'm glad you weren't hurt."

"Me, too," Timmy chimed in.

Bill laid her hand on mine. "We all are."

Timmy cleared his throat and glanced down at the floor. "I told Bill about the twenty dollars."

For some reason, I wasn't surprised, but I was mighty proud of my nephew. I looked at Bill.

With a smile, she nodded briefly. "Looks like you were right."

"About what?"

She nodded to Timmy. "About children."

Her uncle snorted. "Well, blazes, girl. Stop talking about whatever it is you're talking about and invite him over for Sunday dinner like you said you would."

Her face turned crimson. "Uncle Hewitt!"

I felt my ears burn, but I knew that wouldn't keep me from Sunday dinner.